"Are you afraid," he said softly, "that we would end up in bed together?"

Her eyes shot open. "No!" she lied in an awful squeak.

"Then you have no reason to refuse," he said, casually peeling a leaf.

"I don't know...."

"Do this, or I'll see to it that our divorce takes years to settle," he said in a steely tone. Her heart sank. He meant every word—and had the money and power and ruthlessness to carry out his threat.

with his tongue. The magic of his fingers, tantalisingly laborious as they undid the ties of her briefs, ensured that she did forget. The glorious surrender of her body began. Throatily whispering outrageous things to her, describing in detail what he had in mind, Dimitri eased her gently to the warm teak deck.

Her hands clutched at the waistband of his swimming trunks and slid them from his body. Beneath her avid fingers, the muscles of his small buttocks contracted and she ran her hands lovingly over the firm curves.

As a lover he was insatiable. Sometimes his hunger startled her, but she, too, could be as wild and demanding. Then there were times, like now, when his tenderness made her heart contract and his thought for her pleasure knew no bounds.

Olivia began to lose control as Dimitri's wicked fingers slipped with unnerving accuracy to the swollen bud of sensation that lay close to her liquefying core. He did love her, she thought in an ecstatic haze. He'd married her, hadn't he?

That evening, with the great ball of a startling red sun hovering low in the sky, she, Dimitri and the recently widowed Marina sat drinking strong Greek coffee on the terrace of Dimitri's mansion overlooking Olympos Bay.

Marina had been sour-faced ever since they'd returned, glued to one another like limpets, after their day out. Olivia's heart had sunk at the sight of the woman. It wasn't easy, having your hostile mother-in-law living with you! Yet she knew how lonely Marina was since her husband's recent death. She had known such loneliness when her parents had been killed in a motorway accident.

In a friendly gesture, she touched her mother-in-law's arm with a sympathetic hand—which was almost immediately removed. Unseen by Dimitri, Marina gave her a glowering glance of deep suspicion.

'It's a wonderful sunset,' Olivia said, offering the olive branch of peace in an opening gambit and refusing to be put off.

'It always is,' came the slightly tart reply. 'I suppose you two are leaving me alone tomorrow as well. I remember you are shopping in Athens—'

'Ah.' Dimitri replaced his cup in the saucer.

Olivia knew from the look on his face that he was going to cancel their trip. This would be the third time—and he'd said that he wouldn't disappoint her again.

'Not business!' she protested.

It seemed to her that he squirmed a little. 'Some local… meeting that I can't avoid. And after that I must fly to Tokyo for a week. Sorry. I'll make it up to you.' His smile was perfunctory, as if his thoughts were elsewhere. 'When I return, we'll definitely hit the shops and wear our credit cards out—'

'I'm not a child to be offered bribes in pacification,' she said, hurt. So he was going away again. Misery swept over her.

'No. But this is important. In fact,' he said, rising, 'there are some calls I have to make in preparation—'

'Minions,' she muttered, glowering.

Dimitri paused in mid-stride as he headed for the door. He was anxious to call Athena to see if her false labour pains had really gone away, and he didn't take kindly to Olivia's resentment.

Turning slightly, he gave her a long, steady look. She didn't understand. She had everything: money, a husband and security. In contrast, poor Athena had so little—though he'd make damn sure she didn't go short. He himself had known poverty, and the enervating fear that went with it. When it was born—any time now—Athena's child would carry Angelaki blood in its veins. He would have protected her and her child even if he hadn't promised his dying father that he would do so.

Athena had given Theo, his father, the love and warmth that had been lacking in his marriage. Dimitri had seen his father's new happiness with his young mistress and, though his feelings had been mixed, he had been pleased for him. But he would keep his oath that his mother would never know the humiliating truth. It was a matter of honour—and respect for his mother's feelings.

Preoccupied with Athena's immediate need for reassurance and security, he felt irritation rising at Olivia's apparent dissatisfaction with life.

'Remember that because of my hard work you are enjoying the proceeds of my wealth,' he shot back angrily, and stalked into the mansion.

Seething at that unfair stab, Olivia sat tight and sipped her coffee. She wanted Dimitri, not his millions. Until her marriage she'd always worked, and had always occupied her mind. Now she was experiencing boredom for the first time in her life as she whiled away day after day, waiting for him to come home.

That wasn't healthy. No wonder she pounced on him when he returned from yet another trip. Her Greek wasn't good enough to win her a job to give her an outside interest—not that Dimitri would let her work.

His mother ran the house and gardeners tended the grounds so all Olivia could do was to sightsee and shop. And long for Dimitri's return when the house and she would spring into life again.

Paradise, she reflected, had its downside. She stared unhappily at the million-dollar view. The sun, now a yellow furnace, slipped beneath the horizon. For some reason she felt close to tears. And suddenly homesick for her friends.

'My dear!' exclaimed Marina with false concern. 'Your first quarrel!'

'We're both passionate people,' she said coolly.

'Dimitri does not like women to argue with him.'

'He knew what he'd got when he married me. We'd worked together and slept together for two years,' she reminded Marina. 'He loves my independence. Loves it when I stand up to him—'

'Oh, *then* he did, yes,' Marina murmured. 'But not now you are his wife. He will expect obedience.'

'He can expect all he likes,' Olivia said tiredly.

'Then you must realise that he will turn to someone soft and yielding. Like his mistress. I expect that's where he's gone now,' Marina said with satisfaction.

'Mistress? He wouldn't have the energy to manage another woman,' Olivia told her with unusual frankness, stung by Marina's spite.

The older woman pursed her lips in disapproval of such intimate knowledge.

'My son is more of a man than you know. I'll give you her address. I think her name is Athena. You can see for yourself.'

A cold chill went through Olivia. That had been said with such certainty... Please, no, she thought. She couldn't bear it. Suddenly she felt she must get away from Marina.

'I'm going to bed. Goodnight.'

Shaking with apprehension, she made her way to the master bedroom, where she found Dimitri lounging on their vast bed, laughing and murmuring into the phone. The moment he saw her he cut the call short and she felt a terrible sick sensation sweeping through her.

They stared at one another like two wary opponents in a boxing ring. She saw disappointment in his eyes before he swung off the bed and strode past her.

'Where are you going?' she asked, hating herself for sounding like a nagging wife.

'Out.'

'At this hour?'

Oh, that was stupid! But she understood now why women probed like this. They didn't trust their husbands. And often with good reason.

He studied her soft, trembling mouth and almost told her. Then he bit back the words that were on the tip of his tongue and said curtly; 'At this hour.' And he strode out before she could weaken him.

Olivia stood in the middle of the luxurious bedroom, mistress of all she surveyed, co-owner of the mansion and all its valuable contents, of a penthouse in Athens overlooking the Acropolis, a Georgian house in Berkeley Square, a yacht, a private jet and apparently unlimited funds. Yet never had she felt so bereft, so shorn of everything she valued.

The wealth and its trappings were nothing without Dimitri's love. If he didn't care, then she had nothing. She looked down at her shaking hands. The huge diamond in her engagement ring flashed at her as if in mockery. The diamond necklace, designed to look like a scattering of glittering daisies at her throat, felt suddenly like a slave's halter.

She was a wife now. A possession. And according to their marriage ceremony she was supposed to stand in awe of her husband. At least, she thought wryly, she'd then been directed to stamp on his foot. Pity she'd just tapped his instep with her toe.

Olivia frowned, remembering that he had been instructed to love her as if she were his own body. All right. Either he did love her or he didn't. She wasn't going to be used purely as a sex object, or a breeding ground for Angelaki children while he 'played away'. At times like this it was sink or swim, and she'd never been the sinking sort.

Her mouth firmed in determination. If he did have a mistress, she would leave him. She would not be shared. Tomorrow she would swallow her pride and ask Marina for that address.

No man made a fool of her. No man would ever use her purely to appease his sexual appetite. Better a life without Dimitri than that.

She noticed that the sprig of lemon blossom she'd placed on the bathroom shelf had withered and died. Was that an omen? She met her own blazing aquamarine eyes and grim mouth in the baroque mirror, the full enormity of her situation striking her with chilling reality. This time tomorrow she could be on the plane back to England.

CHAPTER ONE

IT WAS three years since she'd last been in Athens. Three interminable years since she'd walked out on Dimitri after wrecking their bedroom in a fit of helpless rage, flinging valuable objects around as if they were cheap souvenirs. It had done nothing to ease the searing pain.

He had been cheating on her. She had seen it with her own eyes. Marina had driven her to a small village near ancient Mycenae, just in time to witness Dimitri's tenderness as he shepherded his mistress towards his car.

His hugely *pregnant* mistress. For a moment she hadn't been able to breathe, so great was the shock. The woman was obviously in labour. That—and Dimitri's loving care—hurt more than anything. She felt that she would have preferred to find them both naked and in the act of love. Seeing his devotion to a woman who carried his child had been infinitely worse.

'Believe me now?' Marina had enquired.

And when Marina had driven them away Olivia had known that she'd never be able to forget Dimitri's betrayal.

She had been devastated. Arriving back at the villa, a gloating Marina had reminded her that Dimitri must now be on his way to Tokyo.

'Go home,' Marina had urged. 'To the people who love you.'

'Yes,' she'd whispered, aching for loving arms around her. 'I need my friends.'

Her note to Dimitri had been brief but heartfelt. *When there is no love in a marriage, it is a mistake to continue it.* Yet a little part of her had hoped that their marriage could be saved. Maybe he'd find her in England, to apologise, and beg her forgiveness and they would begin again.

But he had made no contact. It was as though someone had turned off a light inside her. Men seemed pale shadows compared with Dimitri. England was greyer than she remembered and life was less exuberant. Greek life, and one Greek male in particular, had suited her temperament, but she had to move on. And divorce was the first step.

'How are you feeling?' Paul Hughes, her lawyer and friend, solicitously took her hand in his.

She withdrew it on the pretext of tucking a strand of hair back into her tight chignon. 'Ready for battle,' she replied grimly.

'Next month, you could be one of the richest and most powerful women in Europe!' Paul crowed.

Money and power. Was that all men cared about? Why didn't they put love first, like women? She settled back in her seat, crossly smoothing imaginary creases from the figure-hugging skirt of her white linen suit.

Her hand was shaking and she stared at the back of the chauffeur's head, pumping up her courage with cold, clinical anger by thinking of the terrible moment when her love for Dimitri had shattered into bits.

On his yacht, moored near Piraeus Harbour, Dimitri dealt with his e-mails, despatching instructions to his property agents scattered about the globe. Business was doing well—though it should be, since he'd devoted eighteen hours a day to it for the past three years.

Unravelling his six-feet of toned muscle from the confining chair, he escaped from his desk, unable to concentrate, incapable of sitting like a trapped lion for a moment longer. He'd glanced at his watch impatiently. Ten minutes and she'd be here.

She'd been in his mind ever since the call. The scent of her body. The wicked look in her eyes as she wound herself around him, capturing him in her silken web.

'I want a divorce,' she'd said coldly, two days earlier.

'Come and get it, then,' he'd replied, and severed the connection.

He'd sat motionless for an hour, steaming. So many questions had been on his lips. Where have you been? Why run away like a coward? And why the hell did you marry me—for sex and money, as everyone told me over and over again till I doubted even those early months of married bliss? Then had come the most chilling question of all. Did you *ever* care?

He scowled at the glittering sea and wondered why she had waited till now for a divorce. Perhaps she was afraid of his anger. With good reason. Though his mother had said it was because she'd run out of money and that fact had conquered her fear of what he might do to her. It was odd, though. The allowance he paid every month into their old bank account was more than generous.

Sometimes when he lay awake at night he imagined himself putting his hands around that slender neck and throttling her. Or flinging her to the ground and...

He disgusted himself. She'd aroused terrible emotions that shamed him utterly. The raw animal nature of his fury appalled him. He'd believed himself to be a gentleman, but Olivia had reduced him to his basest instincts. Hatred, ungovernable desire and revenge.

His fist descended on his desk with such force that everything on it bounced. He slammed the fist into his palm. His eyes glittered. He was ready.

Taking the stairs three at a time in huge leaps, he emerged onto the deck to find Eleni, the daughter of his business partner. She was outstaying her welcome. He had relented—under persistent pressure from his mother—to take Eleni on a trip along the coast for a couple of days.

With Olivia constantly filling his mind he'd been bad company and Eleni had irritated him beyond belief. Too girly. Too breathless, clingy and starry-eyed. And, at nineteen, too young to be a companion for him anyway. Poor kid.

He took a deep breath to steady his nerves. This meeting with Olivia had to be short and sharp. It would be a merciful release from a marriage that had died with Olivia's curt admission that she didn't love him.

'Time to go,' he announced in crisp tones of authority. 'You're due at your father's for lunch.'

Sulkily, Eleni rose, her bikini-clad silicon-enhanced body voluptuous and tanned, her blonde hair swishing around her shoulders and reminding him sharply of his final day with his wife.

Hating to remember even one second of that deceitful day, he clenched his jaw in anger. It had figured in his dreams as their last perfect time together. Yet all the time they'd been making love she must have been planning her departure. He ground his teeth in impotent fury.

Olivia had made a fool of him and that was unforgivable.

Where she was concerned, their relationship had been nothing but lies, lust and credit cards. Lies he could brush away with contempt. His bank balance could cope with her spending sprees—which he'd encouraged, admittedly, delighting in lavishing gifts on her and watching her slither into fabulous creations by top designers. And out of them again. His hand shook.

But the lust... That was an unbearable loss. Desperate to forget her, he'd made love to several willing women, but they were nothing compared with Olivia. Worse, it crucified him to know that she would be incapable of doing without sex. Through many sleepless nights he'd fumed over his highly coloured imaginings of Olivia writhing beneath some other man. Or men.

Eleni reached up on tiptoe to kiss his cheek. Her mouth seemed to press more firmly than usual and he realised that his fears were real. She was definitely being lined up as his next wife.

Inwardly he cursed as he saw his car approaching the mooring. He'd miscalculated the journey time. Either baggage control had got its act together or the notorious Athens traffic must have been less dense than usual.

'My wife is here,' he said curtly. 'Get dressed and stay out of sight. Go!'

He heard her irritating snigger as she scampered away. Getting rid of a wife was one matter. Acquiring a second bride barely out of her pram before the ink was dry on the divorce papers was another.

As the car had driven into the marina Olivia had identified Dimitri's luxurious yacht immediately—and his tall, arrogant figure standing on the deck. Her heart somersaulted at the sight of him.

But it steadied when she saw his companion. A pneumatic blonde, with hair just like hers and wearing the tiniest of bikinis, was strolling with a hip-swaying walk towards him. The woman was now kissing his cheek and murmuring something sultry in his ear. There was something vaguely familiar about her that she couldn't quite place, as if she'd met her before. Perhaps at a party during their marriage...

'Nice little popsie,' commented Paul.

Olivia's eyes glittered with contempt. Dimitri's mistress had been dark and beautiful with flashing black eyes, another woman entirely. How many dancing girls did he need to fawn over him? She fumed silently. They were all set to discuss divorce and he was intending to parade his latest conquest to show he didn't give a damn!

Well, she'd show him that she didn't care either.

'She's one of Dimitri's *"popsies"*. That's his boat, probably his latest woman, and that's him up there,' she said, proud there was no tremor in her voice.

'Wow. How many million is that worth?' Awed, Paul stared at the luxury yacht, then more warily at the intimidating figure of Dimitri.

'No idea, but he worked for every penny of it,' she said shortly. 'Dragged himself up from nothing, from shepherd's son to property magnate. Worked night and day without ceasing, pitting his brains against the sharpest knives in the box and coming out top through drive, determination and sheer force of personality.'

'Sounds as if you admire the pants off him,' Paul commented sulkily.

Insulted, she turned brightly sparking eyes on the

lawyer. 'I loathe every hair on his head! I'd sooner lie in a pit of venomous snakes and be eaten by rats than be in a room with him!'

Olivia drew in a breath and controlled her temper. She must stay calm. Be dignified. In the privacy of her small flat, she'd rehearsed the right words till she was hoarse.

When she reached the top of the gangplank, regal and icy-featured, she waited for Dimitri to move towards her. Infuriatingly, he just stood like a rock in that conceited way he had, with his legs planted apart, the darkness of his hair and the bright blaze of his obsidian eyes giving her a jolt of surprise.

Long-neglected embers startled her even more by sizzling into life within her. She felt the wonderful, warm, curling sensation in her stomach with some dismay. The hunger was still there, then. Festering like a disease.

Deliberately she put the lid on it. But she still reeled from the impact of Dimitri's magnetism, the lurking strength of his torso beneath the crisp white shirt that was belted neatly into the sand-coloured trousers, and the intense masculinity of his cynical mouth that had once roamed over her body so freely and with such devastating effect.

Her eyes narrowed behind the concealing sunglasses as she surveyed him. She noticed the air of wealth that hung about him and how beautifully groomed he was—in contrast to Paul's drooping and travel-worn appearance.

A glorious hunk of a man. Supremely male and with a raw and magnetic appeal that still had the ability to reach deep into her and stir her senses.

Dimitri was a power to be reckoned with, a man

whose huge personality and vitality could fill a room and draw all eyes. A man in a million.

The air sucked from her lungs, her mouth became dry. Paul, perhaps thinking she was nervous, put his hand in the small of her back and propelled her forward. She had to either go with the flow or stumble, and naturally she chose to move—but silently cursed Paul for giving Dimitri the advantage.

'This is Paul Hughes, my lawyer,' she said coolly and without preamble.

Eyes mocking her, Dimitri nodded with cool indifference and turned away to pick up a towel from the deck, thus neatly ignoring Paul's outstretched hand.

Seething with irritation that this was not going as she'd planned, she glared at the back of Dimitri's head. The raven hair had been cut with its usual precision, the band of olive-toned skin below the sharp black line being a tempting contrast against the crisp edge of his hand-tailored shirt. And his back... Tingles skittered across her skin as she contemplated the gorgeous, so-touchable triangle...

Enjoyed by other women now. That nubile blonde was waiting somewhere below, perhaps waiting for Dimitri's sensitive fingers to arouse her to frenzied delight. A terrible stab of jealousy lacerated her chest.

She heard Paul clearing his throat and found herself jumping in with both feet and firing off her first salvo before the lawyer had a chance to speak. Unfortunately it wasn't what she'd intended to say, but a question she just had to ask before it burned its way out in an unladylike screech.

'Was that your *secretary* I saw you with just now?' she asked coolly.

Immediately he was flung back in time. He saw

Olivia entering his office for her interview as his secretary. Slender and shapely, she had oozed sensuality
despite the modest beige suit and cream shirt, and her
entirely proper demeanour. It was her eyes that had
enticed him, as deep and as mysterious as the sea. And
her mouth, with its high arch and full lower lip, had
made him wonder what it would be like to have her
kneeling before him with that soft mouth sucking the
sweetness from him, that white-blonde hair soft beneath his fingers...

He'd never forget the interview, during which he had
become so heated that he'd opened the windows and
called for a fresh carafe of water. And he had known
that, whatever her secretarial skills, he must have her.

Amazingly she was as efficient as she was beautiful.
Images of her as his secretary filled his brain. The pal-
pable tension as she took his hurried dictation. Then he
saw her spread across his desk, her eyes and fabulous
body reeling him in as he slowly removed her clothes
with shaking fingers.

His jaw tightened, his chest cramping. Enough. It
was over. He turned then, his eyes narrowed as he
thrust his hands into his pockets in a belligerent gesture.

I know your game, he thought. He'd employed it
often enough himself in business not to recognise it.
Disconcert your quarry. Throw them off balance. Find
their Achilles' heel. And she knew all too well that the
sex they'd had together was so incredible that recalling
it would heat him up in seconds.

The same, he thought callously, went for her. Two
could play. But he'd win this one.

'No. Not...my secretary,' he murmured, giving her
the benefit of a long, memory-filled stare.

The richness of his deep voice filled the very air between them with provocative resonances and she felt something inside her give a little shimmy of guilt-laden delight. The curl of his mouth captured her gaze and she had to force herself to remain outwardly cool to hide the oven-heat within.

'Just some woman, then,' she said dismissively.

Did he detect a note of jealousy? he wondered. Mocking amusement flickered in Dimitri's satin-soft eyes. She hadn't recognised Eleni. But then, she had known her before the girl had increased her bust size to its current oversized proportions, dyed her hair and spent some of her father's fortune on liposuction.

'Last time I looked, she was,' he agreed in a sexy drawl, his mouth upwardly curved with salacious, masculine pleasure.

And he let his gaze wander. Linger. Contemplate. Then he reached out and removed her sunglasses before she could protest, slipping them into his pocket. Now he could see her eyes. He smiled into them.

'I need to see into your soul,' he explained.

Olivia glared, even as she felt the knife of jealousy stab deeply in her chest. Dimitri was the most sensual man she'd ever known. It occurred to her that maybe he had never been faithful to her, even in the early days. He was a man of huge passions, vast sexual needs. For all she knew, she could have been merely one of many women he enjoyed.

And did Athena know about this blonde—or had he abandoned Athena and moved on to pastures new? Her head whirled. This was the man she'd married—a man apparently with the morals of a stray dog. It hurt to know she'd been so thoroughly deceived. It made her stomach curdle to think of his betrayal. There had been

times when she'd tormented herself thinking of him
playing with his child.

Her eyes gleamed like blue glass in the mask of her
face. 'You are such a bigoted chauvinist where women
are concerned,' was all she could say in icy derision,
without revealing how upset she was beneath her frosty
exterior.

'Olivia—' Paul began uncomfortably.

'Let me have my say!' she snapped, whirling on him
so abruptly that he was forced to take a step back.

Paul put up his hands in surrender, shocked by her
vehemence.

Dimitri knew at that moment that this man would
never satisfy a woman like her, not for a second. She
liked tough men with big passions. A man who could
tame her fiery nature and bring calm and serenity to
her life. Paul might look at her as if she were the nearest thing to the goddess Aphrodite, the Greek Venus,
but he'd bore her to tears in no time at all.

With his mind working like quicksilver, he began to
think, to plot and scheme. There was much he needed
to know—and that would take time. First he'd get rid
of the lawyer. Then he'd inform her that she'd have to
stay in Greece while the case was being processed.

He smiled. He'd turn Olivia inside out and get the
answers he wanted to all those unasked questions that
had plagued him for the past three years. After that
he'd find a way—whatever that might be—to prevent
her from using her predatory claws on another unsus-
pecting man. A threat, perhaps. A clause in the divorce
settlement preventing her from marrying for some
years… He'd come up with something. He always did.

His shoulders squared with resolve. Olivia wouldn't
know what had hit her. She'd be putty in his hands.

CHAPTER TWO

'YOU want a divorce, I understand,' he said amiably enough, motioning them to the sun loungers with an authoritative hand.

In a graceful movement of her supple body Olivia slid onto the thick cushion before she realised she and Paul were now at a disadvantage in the low recliners. Dimitri towered over them both, dominating them and smirking with self-congratulation at his cleverness.

She wanted to slap him. 'As fast as we can arrange it,' she agreed instead with a smile that dripped honey. 'And,' she said, adding the vinegar, 'with as little contact with you as humanly possible.'

Filled with a reckless and rebellious need to unnerve him, she kicked off her high-heeled sandals and wriggled her bare toes, making the pink varnish gleam in the sunshine. Then she leant back and unbuttoned her jacket before languidly lifting her arms behind her head to revel luxuriously in the warm sunshine.

Dimitri allowed himself a moment to devour her. She had elegantly arranged her slender, endless legs so that he could admire their length from her small arched feet to mid-thigh. With the raising of her arms, the swelling mounds of her breasts had lifted to gleam provocatively above her simple scoop-necked white top. Delectable. His senses stirred. She was playing her little game to the hilt and beyond.

Crouching close to her, and with his back to Paul, he slowly raked her body with his gaze, watching her respond, knowing the tell-tale tightening of her thighs and contemplating with drowsy sensuality the peaks of her breasts which betrayed the effectiveness of his hungry glance. Or her avid sexual greed. It didn't matter which, only that she should want him—and be denied.

Aching for her more fiercely than he could remember, he let his eyes meet hers. For a moment he forgot where he was and what he was doing. She dragged him in, her soft blue eyes telling him everything he needed to know.

His heart raced with dangerous thoughts. She claimed she wanted a quick ending to their marriage and the minimum of contact. He was tempted to make her suffer the exact opposite. A kick of excitement jerked at his solar plexus.

Fighting his way clear of the thickened atmosphere around them, he flung her a dazzling grin and put his hand on her shoulder.

'What are you prepared to do to encourage me to do what you want?' he murmured, resisting the urge to slide his fingers somewhere more interesting. Though he stared at the tantalising curves of her breasts, imagining the feel of them as he weighed them in his hands.

'Whatever it t-takes,' she stammered, and he was delighted to see how dry her mouth was and that her voice was husky. Though the slick of her tongue over her lips almost incited him to moistening her mouth in his own inimitable way.

'You always did put your body and soul into your projects, didn't you?' he said in husky contemplation.

'Look,' the lawyer interrupted petulantly from somewhere behind his back, 'can we get on with this somewhere more suitable? We will want a list of your assets—'

'Oh,' Dimitri said with a low chuckle, his eyes riveted to Olivia's softly parted lips. He remembered their taste. The soft plumpness between his teeth. His voice grew thick with desire. 'I think Olivia knows all about my assets.'

'Some of them lie below your belt and are virtually the public property of any good-looking woman who passes,' she scathed.

He grinned and his black eyes seemed to dance wickedly, sending her into a haze of hunger. His fingers had tightened on her shoulder in a grip of possession.

'I can't help being virile. Our sex was extraordinary, wasn't it?' he murmured. 'Entire continents moved. Flames scorched our—'

'Look here—!' began Paul, red-faced with disapproval.

'Come.' Dimitri catapulted himself to a standing position and had the lawyer off the lounger and across the deck before Paul or she knew what had hit them.

'Dimitri!' she called, angrily swinging her legs to the deck.

She'd blown it. For hour after hour she'd practised what she'd say, the carefully chosen invective and scorn, the icy analysis of his flawed character. All to no avail. He'd turned her into a helpless mass of fluttering hormones merely by looking at her. She ground her teeth and balled her fists in fury.

'Don't worry. I'll be back in a moment,' he flung over his shoulder, and she seethed silently at his blithe and carefree attitude.

'Lemonade, madam?'

Still glaring, she jerked her head around and saw a man clad in immaculate whites bearing a silver salver with a crystal jug and two glasses.

Two glasses! Dimitri must have *planned* to get rid of Paul—

'Madam?'

Innate politeness made her rearrange her scowling face. With an apologetic smile, she nodded.

'Yes. Thank you.'

She could handle Dimitri. Her needs were small—just a few home truths, the divorce, thank you and goodbye. Olivia sipped gratefully at the cooling drink and felt her temperature settle down to something closer to normal.

Restlessly she wandered to the rail and stared at the glittering sea. A thousand islands lay out there, and all the beauties of Greece. Nostalgia slipped, uninvited, into her heart and soul. If only he hadn't strayed. She would give everything to live in this lovely part of the world again.

Closing her eyes, she dreamed of the Olympos promontory which floated in the sapphire sea on the coast of the Peloponnese land mass—the large peninsula to the south of Athens. On Olympos, white and pastel-blue houses snuggled companionably in the hollows of gentle hills thick with olive trees and vines.

The dazzling light gave the sandy beaches and classical ruins a startling clarity. Nothing was mild or gentle. All was passion, laughter and high drama, and she, with her explosive passions, had felt at home. The people were friendly to a fault...

She scowled. Too friendly, and too many faults where Dimitri was concerned! And where the devil was he—?

'Olivia. Forgive me for leaving you.'

She jerked her head around. Bursting with vital energy that took her breath away, he came striding towards her. Alone. Instantly suspicious, she turned around completely to glare at him, leaning back against the rail for support. Because she needed it, badly.

'Where is Paul?'

Dimitri smiled to himself, poured himself a glass of lemonade and came to join her, his step ominously cheerful. He tilted his head to one side and listened. So did she, and after a moment she heard the sound of a car revving up. At that moment he beamed with pleasure and replied.

'On his way to New York.'

Her eyes hardened. 'New...*York?*' she gasped. And, sure enough, when she looked across at the quayside, she saw Dimitri's car disappearing around a corner.

'Mmm.' He took a thoughtful sip, his mouth hypnotically glistening. Her tongue tipped her own lips before she could stop it and his gaze lingered there, making her skin tingle with excitement. 'He seemed very keen.'

'I bet. How much did you bribe him with?' she asked sourly, hating him.

'Not a lot,' he admitted happily. His eyes crinkled, making her heart jerk as she remembered the laughter they'd shared, the happiness she'd imagined was theirs alone. 'The price of a first-class plane ticket, accommodation, all expenses—'

'Why?' she asked, loathing him more every second that passed.

Dimitri's eyes widened innocently. 'My lawyer's there.'

'I see. Not, then, because you think you can bully me into agreeing to some underhand scheme you have in mind while he's absent?'

To see his expression, Olivia thought scornfully as

he reacted with shock horror at her suggestion, you'd think there had never been such an honest and trustworthy man in the whole world.

'What a suspicious mind you have!' he objected. 'I thought you'd be pleased I took such immediate action. The two of them can get on with making lists of my assets and come up with some figure agreeable to both sides—'

'I just want the divorce,' she told him with an impatient gesture. 'Nothing else.'

His eyebrows shot up. 'You mean…no money? Property? Jewellery?'

'That's it.'

'Please! Don't insult my intelligence by pretending you aren't interested in a share of my wealth!' he scoffed. 'No woman would turn down the chance to be rich. And no court would allow me to leave you unprovided for.' His lip curled in contempt. 'After all, you've worked hard and waited a long time for your share of my fortune.'

She bristled. 'What exactly do you mean by that?'

'You spun your net and threw it out and caught me,' he said, the low growl stiffened with steel. 'You're here to claim your reward. In order to get rid of you I'm prepared to play along and pay you off. I know you'd relish the independence it would give you—'

'I have that in spades, with or without money,' she retorted, boiling with the insult. 'And I can support myself. I don't need a man to provide for me.'

'Is that the line you're taking?' he scorned. 'You intend to impress the courts with your lack of greed— and they'll reward you handsomely for your modest demands? Whereas you and I know that you are owed something for the almost professional pleasure you've given me in the bedroom, on the floor, against the—'

'*Professional?* I'm not one of your whores, to be paid for her services!' she shot back before he listed every single place where they had made love.

'No?' His insolent stare suggested that she might be. 'That's what it comes down to, Olivia. Dress it up any way you like, but marrying a man for his money is a kind of prostitution.'

'I agree,' she grated, so angry that her too-silky tresses were slipping from their confining chignon and she didn't even care. Hauling in a hard breath, she snapped, 'But for your information, I married you for—'

'Sex,' he said softly and the hairs rose on the back of her neck as her body sprang into life. 'That's all it was. Let's not pretend it was anything else. We were great in bed. And everywhere else.' He grinned wickedly. 'Remember—'

'I don't want to remember anything!' she flamed, hating him for the flood of erotic images that were churning up her body and mind. Hating him, too, for killing even the happy moments they'd spent together and reducing their relationship to one base urge.

Dimitri had never loved her. He'd admitted it at last. *Sex. That was all it was.* Well, now she knew, and the truth hurt her more than she could ever have imagined.

'Nothing?'

His mouth had curved into a shape of such carnality that she felt a shudder of desire ripple through her before she managed to drag her wanton body under control again.

'No! It was all a lie, wasn't it? Those declarations of love. The flowers, the little gifts—and the notes you left lying around for me to find... All part of your seduction technique, honed to perfection on...how many women?' she cried heatedly. 'Oh, there must have been hundreds! It was so slick, so smooth! You've probably fathered bastards all over Greece. New York too, for all I know! You humiliated me with your cheating and lying and it gave me great pleasure to disappear off the face of the earth so that you couldn't marry some other deluded female and cheat on her, too!'

Oh, help, she thought. Whatever had happened to her intended cool condemnation of him? Her speech had gone clean out of her head. He just made her *mad*, that was the trouble.

'Me? Cheat?' He frowned as though he didn't know what she was talking about. And then his face tightened. 'I see. You've realised that you are on shaky legal ground in saying there was no love in our marriage. You intend to claim in court that you walked out on me because I was unfaithful.'

'*Claim?*' she stormed. 'Don't insult my intelligence! If you're going to pretend you're as innocent as the driven snow then you're more of a louse than I imagined!'

His scathing glance stabbed into her. 'If you are prepared to malign my character for your own ends—'

'Malign!' she gasped, flinging her head up in outrage and scattering the remaining pins that had held her hair in place. 'I couldn't make your character any worse if I flung it into a sewer and stuffed it full of dead rats!'

It was typical that even at the height of his anger he was able to find her outburst amusing. Their brief, fire-brand rows had always ended in laughter, usually prompted by some outrageous overstatement on her part. And after the laughter had come the making-up...

'Always a colourful phrase on the tip of your tongue,' he drawled, shutting his mind to their passionate reconciliations. The darkness returned to his eyes. 'But I warn you not to make false accusations against me.'

'I won't,' she said grimly, and he nodded as though he'd won a victory. She didn't enlighten him. Her evidence of his infidelity might be needed to secure her the divorce. If so, she'd use it. 'I don't want to discuss your sordid life. I have no interest in it or the way you ran rings around me,' she said coldly. 'Now I'm calling the shots and I want rid of you. As soon as possible. Get that?'

'Your eyes are almost violet with rage,' he mused. 'And you're so flushed, I could almost imagine—'

'Don't try to flirt with me!' she jerked, furious at his murmuring tones.

An innocent, piratical lift of his eyebrow sent a quiver through her. 'I can't help—'

'No. Because you don't value women as people in their own right,' she said, scorn in every line of her uplifted face. Dimitri had never been helpless in the whole of his life. 'You see them as potential conquests and you spin them a line, expecting them to lie down and beg. It's just a knee-jerk reaction to you, isn't it?'

'*Knee?* Wrong place, Olivia,' he murmured. 'Try a little higher up.'

Impatiently she flicked her hair back from where it had tumbled seductively over one eye during her outburst. 'Listen to me. Simple words. Simple solution. I want a divorce. You arrange it—fast.'

'But there is so much to discuss!' he protested. 'Your lawyer's talking of a fifty-fifty division which—'

'He has no right to!' she cried, quivering with indignation.

'Really?' he drawled. 'Sorry, Olivia, but I can't believe he'd take it on himself to decide what settlement you deserve. You'll play the sweet, downtrodden and betrayed wife and tell the courts one thing whilst pushing my legal team for as much as you can get in your greedy little hands.'

Dimitri's mouth had taken on a cynical sneer. She felt like thumping him—and Paul. Dimitri clearly didn't believe her protests and thought she was here for a hefty share of his money. Paul had reinforced that opinion.

Silently cursing the lawyer for launching his own agenda, she decided that Dimitri could wriggle for a while, fearing the ruination of his empire. Serve him right. He'd find out the truth for himself when the time came.

'I just want to be free of you,' she emphasised.

'Come clean, Olivia, and then we can deal. I know that you won't expect to go away empty-handed, not after all the effort you put into driving me so crazy with lust that in a weak moment I proposed marriage in order to keep you,' he reasoned.

Olivia bristled. 'Oh, you were incapable of rational thought, were you?'

'As I said, bewitched. And as you well know.' Their eyes met and she felt herself in danger of falling under his spell, as she had that first day she'd walked into his office and the world had spun around her. 'I feel I owe you something though,' he added. 'You've taught me a lesson.'

'Which is?' she asked unsteadily.

'That I'm not a good judge of women when my loins are on fire,' he growled.

A silence fell between them. Olivia struggled to keep her head. Dimitri was weaving his old magic over her and yet she hated him as much as ever. The pressure of the atmosphere seemed to increase and she found herself fighting for breath. Infuriatingly, Dimitri wasn't affected at all, because he broke the heavy silence and spoke quite casually.

'Tell me. What will you do when you are a free woman again?'

'Start a new life,' she shot back, her entire demeanour daring him to obstruct her goal.

'With Paul?' he queried.

'What's it to you?' she demanded.

Everything, he thought, raked with hatred for any man who might look desperately into those sultry blue eyes and slide into her hot little body. He managed a shrug, which gave him time to swallow away the harsh rage filling his throat.

'I'd hate you to be frustrated.'

'No chance,' she assured him, and was surprised to see the flash of anger that lit his eyes.

'So he excites you?' he said, sounding faintly belligerent.

'Good grief! I'm not discussing my personal life,' she replied airily, and half turned, only to be halted when his hand closed firmly around her arm.

'He's very interested in my money—and how much you'll eventually win,' he purred silkily. 'Tell me, Olivia. I need to know…was that what drove you to marry me? Was it a bonus that there was the prospect of good sex? Did you think we'd have fun for a short while, till you struck out for independence and wealth when you judged you could legally sever our bonds? If so, I admire your single-mindedness, your tenacity and patience—if nothing else—for playing the long game.'

How could he believe that of her? It suggested that he held a very cynical view of women—and her in particular. It was outrageous to suggest she'd married him with a view to a lucrative divorce. Vile-minded rat. Deeply insulted, she picked off his fingers one by one, her mouth tight with contempt.

'You don't know me at all,' she snapped.

'I know you well enough to realise that Paul is only half the man you need,' he bit.

'At least he's not the philandering kind,' she countered.

He grinned. 'I agree. He hasn't, if you'll pardon the expression, got the balls.' It pleased him when her mouth twitched in amusement, acknowledging that he was right. 'He might have a fight on his hands.'

She looked up at him in alarm. 'What...do you mean?'

Dimitri gave a low laugh. 'Oh, not that I'll challenge him to a duel for you. I'm not interested in having a whore for a wife—'

'I'm not!' she yelled, pink with indignation.

'Matter of opinion. No, I could contest the divorce. Make things difficult for you.'

'That's spiteful and beneath you,' she croaked.

'Mm. It might be in my interests, though,' he mused. 'What will I get out of legally severing our marriage—other than a halving of my fortune?'

'Freedom,' she told him, agitated.

'I have that,' he told her. 'I do what I like.'

He always had. 'To remarry?'

'Maybe I don't want to.'

'You want children,' she said bluntly. 'Even you can't create blood heirs without the help of a woman. And however many you father on the wrong side of the blanket, I know you would want at least some of your children to be legitimate. It's definitely to your advantage to divorce me so don't pretend it isn't.'

He smiled. 'You're trying to tell me you're doing me a favour?'

'Well, we can't go on like this, being neither single nor married!' she said crossly. 'I want out of this relationship, Dimitri. I want to wipe you from my shoes, where you've been for these past three years, and never see or think of you again. You have influence. See to it that we're divorced quickly. You can play the field all you like then with a free conscience—that's the little voice in your head that tells you when you're doing something morally wrong, by the way,' she added scathingly.

He smiled, clearly amused by her stinging jibe. 'I don't think a divorce will instantly erase me from your memory,' he purred.

A shudder rippled through her in acceptance of the fact that he himself had made too powerful an impact to be forgotten. Somehow she turned it into a shudder of disgust.

'I sincerely hope it does,' she said stiffly. 'Now. This divorce—'

'Ye-e-s. There's a little snag, though. It will take some time, I'm afraid,' he said with feigned regret.

'Then pull some strings.' She wasn't falling for that one.

He shrugged as if he had none to pull. 'I made some

preliminary enquiries after you rang. The courts are overburdened with work.' Reaching forward to lift back strands of hair which had blown across her face, he came closer, his breath reaching her in a tantalising whisper that caused chaos in her frantically thudding heart. 'I hope you realise that you'll need to stay here while the proceedings are taking their course.'

'That's ridiculous!' she cried. 'I'm flying back to-morrow morning—'

'As you like. But there'll be no divorce. If work's a problem—'

'No.' She frowned. 'It's not. Just that I don't want to stay anywhere near you—'

He shook his head as if in regret. 'It's your choice, of course. There are officials to see, papers to sign... You'd never believe the complications. Even if you stay, it could be three or four months before our case even gets onto the list. Then there might be a year's wait while—'

'A year? That can't be right!' she protested, closing her eyes in dismay.

'Would that be a problem?' he murmured. 'Staying here, discussing each stage with me...'

She couldn't do that. Even now his seductive voice was creating havoc within her. It felt to her as though she might drown. Her senses were taking over. Dimitri's eyes had been as liquid as her bones. Every bit of her was screaming for a sexual release—a kiss, a touch, to be crushed in his arms...

Olivia floundered, trying to keep her head above water. It wasn't over between them, she thought bleakly. She hated him. Despised him. Yet the terrible bond was as strong as ever.

'I could, perhaps,' came his voice perilously close

to her mouth, 'hurry things along a little…if I so wished.'

She gulped and surfaced, opening her eyes to find that he was kissing-close, his head already angled as if he was contemplating his assault on her mouth. The drowsiness of his eyes and the sultry set of his lips sent any rational sense to the four winds.

Ruthlessly she gritted her teeth and reminded herself that he'd be unbearable if she ever let him touch her again. He wasn't worthy enough to clean her shoes, let alone have access to her body. Adulterer. Man of few morals… She searched for words to strengthen her resolve. Yes, she thought grimly, and with the self-restraint of a rutting stag!

'Then wish. Find a four-leafed clover, a black cat, a fairy godmother—I don't care, but *wish!* Bribe someone if necessary, but hurry everything up,' she told him, her tone deliberately acid.

His smile would have beguiled her in times long past. He took her glass from her trembling hand and put it, with his, on the table beside the loungers. Then he took her hands in his, moving his thumbs rhythmically over her skin. And all she could do was to look at him, washes of warm heat turning her body into a glowing furnace.

'I'll do that,' he agreed.

'Good,' she husked.

'For a price,' he said thickly.

Her body slumped. Yes. If it's sex, she thought in a crazy moment of weakness, she'd say yes. One last moment together before she shut down her hunger for him and became celibate again.

How awful! she thought, appalled by her feebleness. What was she thinking?

Despairing, she fought her appallingly wayward, abandoned nature and tried desperately hard to remain indifferent. But he had taken her in his arms now and his body almost touched hers. Every inch of her wanted to strain forward so she could feel the hard, muscular torso against the softness of her breasts and enjoy the pressure of his narrow hips as his pelvis settled against hers.

'I won't pay your price!' she croaked. They fitted so well. Always had. Her head spun.

'I think you will,' he countered with soft certainty.

He was exultant. Her arousal had astonished him. But then they'd always matched one another in their demands. No doubt Paul had starved her of true satisfaction. He had a powerful urge to erase her lovers from her mind and body.

She would definitely pay the price he demanded. He'd see to that. Dimitri touched her quivering mouth, a knife-wound of excitement shafting through him when she gave a little gasp. Oh, yes. To have that glorious body in his bed, to remind her how good their sex had been, that would ease his ache. He would keep her until she didn't know which way up she was. And then when she was utterly dependent on him he'd dump her so fast her feet wouldn't touch the floor.

But hell. He wanted her. *Now!* For the time being, a quick retreat might be wise.

'Wait there. I'll see what I can come up with,' he whispered. And couldn't resist touching her lips with his, intending the kiss to be brief and casual.

Yet in seconds they were wrapped around one another. The ferocity of their passion startled even him. A warning voice in his head told him that he must get away before he showed his desperation.

'Mm. Very nice. But I have a call to make.' Everything throbbed. His blood raced around his body, turning his head to mush. He pushed a hand through his hair and steadied himself, mentally, physically and emotionally. 'I will see what I can do to speed things up.'

Somehow he found his way to the cabin door, though he felt as intoxicated as a drunk. But then he was addicted to her and the more he had the more he wanted. This time, however, it would be on his terms and he would be emotionally detached. The safest way, where his harlot wife was concerned.

Not for nothing did he come from 'under the ditch', the ditch being the pet name for the Corinth Canal that cut off the Peloponnese peninsula from the Greek mainland and turned it into a technical island. People from his area were considered to have a particularly devious mental agility. They could assess a situation and turn it to their advantage, which was why so many Greek politicians came from his homeland.

He headed for the salon, his brain fizzing as if it had been plugged into a socket, his body vibrantly alive. An idea had come to him of such startling simplicity that it left him breathless. He'd deal with Olivia and the Eleni problem at the same time.

A sense of elation made him want to shout and he caught himself grinning stupidly. He'd have one hell of a roller-coaster ride with Olivia. By the time he'd finished with her, she'd be begging him to let her stay as his wife and she would know for herself the humiliation and pain of being rejected. And he'd make sure she realised that he'd treated her like the callous little tramp she really was.

CHAPTER THREE

FOR a moment or two after Dimitri had disappeared into the cabin, Olivia remained at the rail, clinging on to it for dear life because her legs were in no fit state to do the job for which they'd been designed.

No wonder she hadn't been interested in those other men who'd been keen to take her out. Over the past couple of years she'd accepted a few invitations to dinner, hoping that she could forget Dimitri in some other man's arms. All too soon she had discovered that the experimental dates had only reinforced the hold Dimitri still had on her.

Being with him again was like leaping into a maelstrom of emotion and feeling, where her senses became heightened and every cell in her body hummed and vibrated as if they'd been connected to a power source.

She paced the deck, horrified by her arousal and deeply ashamed that her sexual hunger could override her contempt for Dimitri. He really imagined that she'd leap into bed with him, given the chance—and perhaps she might, she thought with a groan.

Hearing him flinging open the cabin doors again, she spun around, her heart pounding at the sight of him, his passionate eyes dark and unwavering as he strolled towards her trembling body.

'I can offer you a quickie if you like.' He smiled at her, one eyebrow lifted in query.

Olivia inhaled sharply and raised her hand to slap his face but he caught it, laughing, the sudden crinkling of his eyes and the warmth of his expression making her knees liquefy.

'How dare you?' she whispered.

'Sorry. Your language sometimes has too many meanings. I meant a quickie divorce,' he said, amused.

Sceptically she narrowed her eyes. Dimitri knew exactly what he'd said. His English was impeccable. If she'd gone all coy on him, he would have grabbed her and rushed her down to his cabin without a second thought. Though what the pneumatic blonde would think of that, she wouldn't know. It shocked her that Dimitri could juggle two women, only a few feet from each other, without turning a hair!

'Do it, then,' she said coldly, snatching her hand free.

'And you'll agree to what I want?'

'Not to anything illegal or immoral!' she declared.

'Absolutely not,' he said, sounding prim and shocked. She stared at him witheringly and he grinned again. 'Well?'

'Depends. I can think of several things I *won't* do for you.' Her wary eyes searched his and met a wall of blandness.

'Don't worry. It's something well within your capabilities,' he said, not calming her suspicions at all. 'I'll explain to you over lunch.' He motioned her to the cabin but she stayed put.

'Is this a pretext to get me into your cabin and your bed?' she asked, trying to keep a rein on her runaway desires.

'Is that a round-about way of asking?' he enquired silkily.

A flush spread from her neck to the roots of her hair. 'It certainly isn't!'

'Uh-huh.' He didn't sound too convinced.

'I loathe you, Dimitri. Do you honestly think I'd want to slip between the sheets with you?' she derided.

His shoulders lifted in a typically Greek shrug. 'It doesn't have to be sheets. I have a very wide desk... Still,' he hurried on, seeing her furious expression, 'it looks as if I must settle for lunch and a discussion, then. Hungry?' he asked.

She blinked. It was hours and hours since she'd eaten, her nerves preventing her from touching breakfast—or even her meal the night before. There was no point in starving. And Dimitri always ate well. He had the most wonderful chef who prepared sumptuous meals for when he was on the boat. Her mouth watered.

'I could eat a horse,' she admitted.

'I think we can come up with something a little less controversial than tucking into one of our equine friends.'

Olivia almost smiled at his dry comment, but stopped herself in time when she remembered that the blonde was hanging around somewhere and they might not be alone. There was safety in numbers, but she wasn't too keen on watching Dimitri play footsie under the table with one of his gooey-eyed groupies.

He picked up her shoes and politely handed them to her, then led the way to the cabin.

Olivia felt suddenly nervous. 'Will your blonde... *friend* be joining us?'

Dimitri pulled a face. 'Not if I can help it.' He put out his hand to help her down the steps but she ignored it.

'Not into threesomes, then?' she said sarkily.

'No. Are you?' he enquired.

Her glare answered him. 'I don't particularly want

to meet one of your…popsies,' she began, her mouth twitching when Dimitri roared with laughter at her choice of words. 'But it seems rude to eat separately—'

'Believe me,' he said as they moved into the panelled dining room, 'I want to stay separated from…the popsie. She's the reason I need your help. One of the crew is discreetly putting her ashore now we're in the dining room.'

Callous brute, she thought, feeling a little—only a little—sorry for the woman. She supposed that Dimitri was used to shuffling his mistresses around in order that they never met. How tacky.

They'd eaten their *mezedhes*, choosing delicacies from the countless small dishes of tempting snacks, and had been served with a beautifully presented dish of red mullet before Dimitri ended his non-stop commentary on the delights of Greek cooking.

She'd listened patiently, sipping champagne with the strangely loud notes of a haunting Greek folk tune swirling about them noisily from a hidden music system, and wondering when he'd get to the point.

During his monologue, Dimitri had leaned confidentially towards her. Because of the deafening music she had been forced to do the same, so that she could hear what he'd said. It had given an uneasy intimacy to the meal.

The haunting notes of the bouzouki filled her head and stirred her emotions. She wondered if that was deliberate and she tried to remain unaffected, but it was difficult with Dimitri's handsome face so close, the faint scent of aftershave lingering in the air whenever he threw back his head and laughed.

The waiter deftly slipped dishes of artichokes, courgettes and green beans beside each of their plates and then exited, discreetly closing the door. She almost felt like calling him back, because being alone with Dimitri seemed increasingly risky.

The tender flesh of the fish seduced her tastebuds but Olivia instantly adopted a businesslike air and broke in on Dimitri's lyrically sensual praise of the dish. Before she knew it, he'd be moving from food to other things…

'I have to check in to my hotel this afternoon. There isn't enough time for a tour around Greece's gastronomic delights,' she rebuked. 'Tell me what you want me to do in exchange for a quick divorce. And don't suggest sex. You can find that elsewhere.'

In a leisurely movement, Dimitri leaned back in his chair, eyeing her over the rim of his flute. He looked very satisfied with himself.

'You could get me out of a difficult situation,' he said casually. Olivia popped a forkful of green beans into her mouth and made no comment. Dimitri sighed as though the weight of the world lay on his shoulders. 'It's my mother.'

Her lashes flicked up in surprise. She'd thought the blonde was his problem. 'Go on.'

He tried to sound concerned. It wasn't easy when his pulses were hammering with the cleverness of his plan and every inch of him surged with hard-to-suppress excitement. Carefully he produced a frown and another sigh.

'Once I am a free man she wants me to marry a suitable woman—'

'As opposed to an unsuitable one like me,' Olivia said drily.

'I've never understood why you two have never got on,' he told her. 'The fact is, all these years she's been hassling me to trace you, to divorce and remarry and to provide heirs for the Angelaki empire.'

'You…didn't search for me at all?' She sounded surprised and disappointed.

He scowled, hating to remember that time. Of course he hadn't. She'd made it clear that she didn't love him. What was there to be gained—other than heartache and a series of heated arguments?

With cold precision he had cut her from his heart and sealed up the wound. In time he had found that his anger and frustration eased. And soon he had discovered that his married status kept scheming women and their mothers at bay so that he could get on with burying himself in non-stop work.

'I saw no point,' he replied cuttingly.

Olivia winced. So much for vanity. Yet his indifference hurt. He hadn't even bothered to find her in the hope that their marriage might be saved. That told her how deeply he felt about her—and marriage itself. It confirmed what she'd feared. Dismayed, she hung her head. All she could do was make a quick exit and try to forget that he'd ever shared her life. That seemed pretty unlikely at the moment. But time healed, so they said.

'I loathe you, Dimitri. Every conceited inch. The sooner I can get away, the better.' It gave her no pleasure to say that. Unsteadily, she met the black satin of his eyes. 'Tell me your price. What you want me to do.'

The tense muscles around his mouth relaxed into a triumphant curve. 'Play a role you've played before.'

Games, she thought, her heart sinking. No. It was actually leaping. Her lower lip trembled. Heaven help her. He wanted her to indulge him with some sex game and she found that thrilling! Somehow she dredged up a disdainful look.

'Secretary?'

His grin was deliberately lecherous. 'You fancy trying my desk out after all?'

'Don't flatter yourself,' she muttered, though the pulses in her body were urging her to do just that. 'And I'm not wandering about with a spiral-backed notebook and sitting down with my skirt hoiked up so you can relive some of your lurid fantasies.'

'The thought of you taking dictation while I ogle your legs is certainly an attractive idea,' he admitted, 'but that's not what I have in mind—for now.'

She didn't like the 'for now'. 'What, then?' she asked ominously.

'Unfortunately my mother has found a suitable woman to be my next wife. A young Greek heiress.'

Olivia felt a tremor of shock run through her. Was that why he needed her help with Miss Pneumatic?

'Not…the blonde you hid in a cupboard somewhere on board?'

'Eleni, yes,' he replied, suppressing a smile. 'Don't you remember her? The daughter of Nikos Kaloyirou, my late father's business partner—'

'I do!' she said in surprise. 'And I remember him. Very aristocratic but an absolute sweetie.'

Dimitri grinned. 'He spoke highly of you, too.'

Her puzzled frown cleared. 'Are you saying that the woman I've just seen is little Eleni? She…' Olivia remembered the girl's large nose and chin, and how as a teenager she'd hung around Dimitri as if he was God's gift to womanhood. 'She looks so different now!' she declared in amazement.

The flat chest and heavy hips had gone. Eleni looked fabulous.

'Courtesy of a good surgeon and a doting father. But...' He paused and gave a grimace, shaking his head.

'Don't tell me she doesn't appeal,' Olivia said in disbelief. The woman was gorgeous, right up Dimitri's street. He'd kissed her, too...

'Oh, physically she looks stunning,' he replied, making her entire body tense up with crippling jealousy. 'But that isn't enough, as I learnt from the experience with you.' He flashed her a disarming smile, which she returned with a look of withering scorn.

'If she's that gorgeous, what's wrong with marrying her and having mistresses?' Olivia asked tartly. He'd done that before, after all.

He raised his eyes to the ceiling. 'Everything. She's giggly and stupid and I'd end up throttling her. I'd hate my children to inherit her simpering ways and butterfly brain. My children will need to be quick-witted to run the Angelaki business—and to fob off fortune-hunters. You see my predicament.'

Again he produced a dazzling grin. She felt puzzled. It wasn't just the way Dimitri kept smiling at her but something she couldn't quite fathom. Mischief lurked in his eyes.

She remembered how he'd once told her of a property coup in which he'd outsmarted several high-powered rivals. He'd been the same then, simmering with a very appealing elation that had made his eyes dance as they were dancing now. Her suspicions deepened.

'What happened to your acclaimed art of persuasion?

Can't you use your famed diplomatic skills?' she suggested cynically.

'I *am* using them—by using you, Olivia,' he silked. 'Let's keep our prejudices out of this. You need something and so do I. We can do one another a favour. I want to let Eleni down gently, without insulting my friend and partner and causing a rift that would damage the business. Family honour is a very serious matter to a Greek. I can't appear to insult Eleni. My partner would be obliged to split with me and that could cause mass staff redundancies and ruin many lives.'

'So where do I come in?' she asked, frowning at him from beneath lowered brows.

He beamed back at her, the brightness of his eyes intensifying. 'You already know that you will need to be resident here while the divorce proceedings are being dealt with. During that time you can make yourself useful.'

'Oh, as in warning her off, you mean?' Her eyes gleamed. 'I could tell her what a terrible husband you were. How you left me to the mercy of your mother's viperish tongue and jetted about the world trying out the springs on other women's beds—'

'No thanks, I think I'd prefer something that leaves my good reputation intact,' he said, laughing.

Olivia shot him an incredulous look. 'Good reputation! Huh. Like what?'

He inhaled deeply then said softly, 'I want you to pretend we've met up and have fallen in love again.'

She stared at him, aghast. 'You're kidding!'

'Never been more serious.'

'But…but that's the most ridiculous thing I've ever heard—!'

'No, Olivia. People would believe it. We could put on a good show—'

'*No!*' She went pale at the thought of the kind of show he envisaged.

'You could throw things at me in private,' he offered, his mouth twitching with a horribly appealing humour.

'I'd find it hard not to throw *up* in public,' she muttered.

He chuckled. 'I'll provide you with medication to prevent that. It'll be worth your while. The quickest divorce in Greek history.'

'That appeals,' she conceded. 'But pretending to love you…!'

'Bizarre thought, isn't it?' he said cheerfully. 'But think of the end result. If I'm willing to suffer *you*, I don't see why you shouldn't suffer *me*.'

She scowled, bridling at his comment. Was she that awful to live with? 'That's because you'll enjoy making me simper over you. Whereas I'll hate every moment.'

Even as she said that, she knew she wasn't being entirely honest with herself. And she knew that her protest had sounded half-hearted.

'Olivia.' Dimitri had put on his most coaxing, satiny voice. And while she knew that he was insincere, she still felt inescapably seduced by it. 'We could do one another a good turn. Perhaps even part without rancour. I need you to agree, to get Eleni off my back. If it seems that we are together once more then Eleni, her father and my mother would have to accept that fact.'

'Would they?'

He leaned forward earnestly, fixing her reluctant gaze with his. 'They couldn't in all conscience come between man and wife,' he argued. 'They would immediately set their sights on some other man. The result would be that Eleni wouldn't lose face and she'd detach herself from me without a showdown. She's a nice enough kid underneath. Just…young, spoilt and raw around the edges. Her feelings would be saved from hurt, and my employees will be secure in their jobs.' His thick lashes lowered and lifted lazily. 'You wouldn't like to see people on the poverty line because you can't be bothered to give this a try, would you?'

'Don't use emotional blackmail on me!' she cried indignantly. 'You'll be telling me next that if I don't agree hundreds of people will be begging for grass cuttings to eat—while entire families throw themselves off high buildings—'

'A slight overstatement.' He chuckled in delight. Olivia was mesmerised by his laughing mouth, and he must have known this because he leaned even closer. 'However,' he murmured, 'I can definitely foresee employment problems if I insult Eleni and her father by rejecting her as a bride. In Greece we defend family honour. As I said, the very least my partner could do would be to cut our business ties, causing untold devastation to the Angelaki empire. You can do this, Olivia—'

'You're wrong! I can't!' she protested, scared stiff of being close to him for any length of time.

Already a wicked little voice was urging her to agree so that she could be with him. Yet she didn't trust her seesaw emotions and had no intention of falling for him all over again.

'You can,' he coaxed. 'It won't be for long. When Eleni is safely off the scene, you can slip away a free woman and never see me again. It won't be a difficult task to pretend you love me.' His tone grew cynical. 'You managed it for six months while we were married, after all.'

Olivia hardly registered that, her brain refusing to move into gear. 'It's…horribly manipulative.'

'Thank you! I'm flattered.' Flashing his white teeth at her again, he raised his glass to her and then drained it.

His mouth was moist and relaxed. Olivia stared at it, mesmerised, imagining them together again. Pretending…

'How…?' She grabbed her own glass and took a hasty gulp to ease the dryness of her throat. 'How long might this take?'

'I'd hope two weeks. Maximum. Take time off work—'

'I'm between jobs,' she said, and could have kicked herself when he beamed.

'No big deal, then, is it? You don't even have to lie about your feelings. Just a puppy-dog look here, a sigh there…' Enthusiastically he tackled the vegetables on his plate, pushing them into the exotic sauce and closing his eyes in ecstasy. 'Bliss,' he sighed and then his black lashes lifted, his eyes burning holes in her.

She had the unnerving impression that he wasn't talking about the food, but the prospect of having her dancing to his tune.

'I don't think so,' she muttered.

'It is. Try it,' he said, choosing to misunderstand her.

His fork hovered close to her mouth. Bemused, she opened her lips before she realised she was playing into his hands. The fish melted in her mouth, the velvety sauce stimulating her tastebuds. Dimitri's eyes melted into hers, stimulating every other sense she possessed.

It seemed that the electrified air sizzled and crackled between them, connecting their bodies in a fatal circuit. Feeling faint, she reached for her glass, realising as she sipped frantically that somehow it had been refilled.

Her head whirled. Whether that was from alcohol or the nearness of Dimitri, she didn't know. Only that she had to cut this cosy tête-à-tête short before she found herself leaning forward a fraction more and...

'Olivia.'

She swallowed as the throaty tones vibrated deep inside her. Music swirled erotically about them, the insistent rhythm eating into her brain. In an agonisingly tender gesture, his hand touched her cheek in a light caress and her eyes closed against her will.

'Are you afraid,' he said softly, 'that we would end up in bed together?'

Her eyes shot open. 'No!' she lied in an awful squeak.

'Then you have no reason to refuse,' he said, casually peeling a leaf from his artichoke and dipping it in butter.

She watched, hypnotised, as he delicately sucked the butter off and slipped the fleshy part of the leaf into his mouth. His challenging smile made her blood boil. He thought she'd be good for a quick lay. The arrogance of the man! Maybe she did keep falling for his practised seduction techniques. But she hadn't actually succumbed.

It would give her the greatest satisfaction to prove that he wasn't the irresistible Lothario he imagined. All she needed to do was to remember he had at least one illegitimate child—and that he thought women were merely toys, designed for his pleasure. That would keep her from making a fool of herself over a man who could well be a serial adulterer.

She hated him, after all.

In genuine disgust, she gave a shudder, as if she was repelled by the thought of spending time with Dimitri.

'My only hesitation is that I'd have to pretend to like you,' she said, grimly attacking her fish, stabbing it with her fork as though it might be his body. 'And what about your mother? She won't be too pleased.'

'She thinks badly of you for leaving me,' he agreed. 'But she must learn that I run my own life. One day I might fall in love. She must be fully prepared to accept the woman I love, whoever and whatever she is. I want my mother's blessing when that time comes.'

Olivia winced. Something tore in her chest. Jealousy, she supposed. Dog-in-the-manger. How small-minded of her. She didn't want him but couldn't bear to think of him being in love.

She wondered if he wanted to marry Athena and legitimise his child. Or if he had grown tired of her and discarded her long ago.

It was hard to think, what with the heavy beat of the music and her scattered wits.

'I don't know…'

'Do this, or I'll see to it that our divorce takes years to settle,' he said in a steely tone.

Her heart sank. He meant every word—and had the money and power and ruthlessness to carry out his threat.

'You are an opportunistic swine!' she muttered.

'That's right.'

It annoyed her that he had the upper hand. It didn't matter to him if they were divorced or not—in fact it had probably kept Eleni from demanding that he set a wedding date. Olivia glowered, feeling like kicking something. Preferably Dimitri. She wanted to get her divorce signed, sealed and delivered so that her new life could begin. Perhaps two weeks swooning over Dimitri wasn't too much to ask.

'I need to think this over.' Suddenly feeling fragile and desperately vulnerable, she pushed her plate away.

'Of course.'

He nodded and they ate their puddings in silence. Or, at least, he did. Trying to remain objective, she toyed with her *bougatsa*, even though it was her favourite dessert, and considered his extraordinary suggestion.

Everything was conspiring to make her say 'yes'. Despite seeing no other way to make him do what she wanted, the music had somehow tapped into her emotions. The food reminded her of the exotic tastes she'd enjoyed so much. And above all, there was that beautiful country waiting outside.

If she did have to remain in Greece for a while then she had to admit that it would be lovely to stay at his mansion, even if she had to play the loving wife to do so. She loved the old Venetian house and had missed it with a deep ache in her heart that had astonished her. But it was perfect. The views across the Saronikos Gulf were spectacular, the furnishings luxurious and comfortable, yet the ultimate in good taste.

Every day she could revisit the places she adored. The little town of Nafplion, with its Venetian houses and fountains and squat fortresses guarding the harbour. The golden beaches and savage crags, the spectacular ruins of ancient Greece and Rome atop verdant hills, every path and stone richer in drama and history than anywhere else in the whole of Greece.

It was the land of Agamemnon and Helen of Troy. Of Hercules, gods and goddesses. Magical.

She thought of the silent glades and crystal-clear rivers, the intoxicating scent of the wild flowers and the inviting warmth of the sea, as deep a blue as her eyes, Dimitri had murmured once.

All this she had lost and mourned because of his infidelity. For two short weeks it could be hers again, to record on her camera and to smile over in future days when the hurt and emotion had become just a distant memory.

'Come.' His hand was on her arm and she was rising blindly, obediently from her seat. 'I think we both need a shot of coffee,' he murmured, guiding her to the salon.

In the doorway he spoke briefly in Greek to the waiter, who was arranging a tray of coffee and chocolate peppermints on a low table inlaid with mosaics. The evocative sound of Maria Callas singing of her lover's betrayal in the opera *Madame Butterfly* filled the room, the plaintive, soaring pure notes reaching deep into Olivia's wounded heart and tearing relentlessly at her emotions.

'Olivia, we don't have much time. Have you come to a decision?' Dimitri asked quietly, turning her around to face him.

She looked up at him and hastily averted her eyes. But she could smell that masculine aftershave and could feel his power energising her. He was too close for comfort. Any moment now and she'd lift her face for a kiss—and be thoroughly humiliated by her lack of sense. Panic jerked at her. Anxious to escape to the safety of a chair, she blurted out suddenly, 'Yes. I'll do it.' And added in defiance, 'For me, not for you.'

He smiled, the corners of his lips curving appealingly. And, oh, she could drown in those velvety eyes. At that moment she panicked, worrying that she'd committed herself to something she couldn't handle.

'For you?'

Aware of the danger she'd risk if she continued to look up at him, she coolly focused on the third button of his shirt. 'Why not?' she replied, miraculously assuming a casual air. 'It'll be a nice holiday. Luxurious surroundings, use of a car—which I insist on—and the chance to explore.'

'I will spare no expense in amusing you,' he drawled. He had been right. She could be bought. Almost every woman had her price, it seemed. Disappointment wiped out his pleasure at having her in his power. 'In return, you must give me your word you'll do this. That you won't back out. I have to know my plan has every chance of succeeding.'

Her eyes flicked up then; the darkest aquamarine like the sea at the mouth of the caves on the east coast of the Olympos promontory. Enticing. Fathomless.

'Shake on it,' he said, more curtly than he'd intended, and he put out his hand. 'Swear that you will see this through to the end.'

'I promise.'

Hesitantly her fingers touched his palm and then her hand had slid into his.

It wasn't what he'd intended—not yet—but he found himself drawing her close until she lay in the circle of his arms. Warning voices were telling him that he could scare her off at this delicate stage, but to his surprise he discovered that he wasn't capable of holding back.

Suddenly they were kissing. Hot, frantic kisses that

burned and seared. Their hands were clutching and possessing, bodies crushed together in a desperate need for every inch to be touched and caressed and relieved of terrible, unsatisfied hungers.

Their mutual lack of finesse startled him, he who'd always been so proud of his skills at wooing a woman and the smoothness of his approach as he coaxed and kissed his way to his goal. But his feelings were overwhelming him, shutting down his brain, his mind focused only on the glorious sensation of her plush mouth on his, her body fitting into him as if they had been made for one another.

His mouth found the soft warmth of her throat and she flung her head back with a groan of sheer pleasure. The shock of her beauty ripped through him. She was so lovely that it hurt, great, scything shafts of pain slicing him from head to toe.

His weight moved her backwards till she hit the panelled wall with a dull thud. Slipping his hand down, he pushed up her skirt and let his fingers enjoy the softness of her thigh. With a little shudder, she raised her leg and hooked it around his back. Hardly able to contain his excitement, he concentrated on lifting her T-shirt over her head.

The languid stretch of her arms made his pulses drum loudly. And she left them raised above her head, open to him, boldly and unmistakably inviting his invasion.

'You are incredibly beautiful,' he whispered, then dipped his head to kiss her scented breasts where they heaped generously above a lacy bra.

He closed his eyes, sensing the arching of her spine, the urgent thrust of her hips, and he responded with a fierce onslaught of impassioned kisses that left him breathless. And more frantic than ever to take her.

Even if she had used him... Angrily he ripped off her briefs and shuddered when she sighed as though in relief and melted against him, her teeth savaging his shoulder, his throat, his jaw...

This was pure sex in its rawest state. And yet he could feel his heart aching for more than that as he let her snatch at his shirt and forcibly wrench it open, scattering buttons in all directions.

Her mouth was moving over his naked torso, driving him wild, the slick of her tongue and the nip of her sharp teeth jerking his body into a frenzy while her hair slid with more tantalising delicacy, reminding him of other times when he had imagined they were making love as a couple who adored one another.

Tormented and tortured with this betrayal, he caught a hank of golden hair and raised her head. Their eyes blazed, liquid jet meeting bewildered sapphire. Something broke in him. His heart, his control, any contact with reality.

Olivia knew this was madness but couldn't stop herself. All her solemn resolutions had been swept away the moment he had taken her into his arms. There was such a joy in her heart when he looked at her and touched her that she knew with an almost chilling certainty that she still loved him and always would. Like an animal craving water, she needed him to make her live again, to make her whole. Without him she was nothing.

Whimpering in a confusing muddle of dismay and delight, she began to drag off her bra with infuriatingly clumsy fingers, almost weeping when the hooks refused to be released. Dimitri reached around her back and yanked it free. Her naked breasts touched his chest tentatively, their dark centres immediately hard and exquisitely painful. She let her body sway a little so that they brushed his quivering muscles, rejoicing in the sound of his quickened breathing.

They would make love. Their feelings for one another had been reignited. It would be like old times, she dreamed.

And all the while his fingers were slipping relentlessly between her thighs, slicking backwards and forwards in a ruthless rhythm that was becoming unbearable.

She touched him. His groan echoed hers when her hand closed around the hot smoothness and suddenly he was impatiently pushing her hands away and was thrusting inside her with an urgency that took her breath away.

It had never been like this before. Never so uncontrolled, so primitive or needy. Her arms locked around his neck and she buried her head in his shoulder, feeling the silken slide of him against each unfurling nerve within her, wondering at the ecstasy and despair that battled in her heart.

Their mouths clashed. Teeth and tongues fought together as all the years of longing and anger welled up within her. She cried out, called his name, heard him huskily whisper hers as his thrusts became faster and more vigorous, wiping away the past and focusing her on the here and now.

Gasping, she felt the rising ripples of an orgasm, enhanced by his skilful, wickedly arousing fingers. On the summit of it, she hovered and began to subside, only to be driven there again and again.

Dimly she was aware of the thick carpet beneath her

back. Then of them rolling, locked in a passionate embrace, unable to release one another till the silken pressure within her had swelled again and they had reached a shuddering climax together.

Slowly the madness faded and she felt calmness descend on her. Limp and glowing with delirious delight, she lay silent and still in Dimitri's arms, dreaming of their renewed love. She had never been so certain of anything in her life. He had been so frantic for her, muttering what had sounded like sweet Greek words of adoration.

With a long exhalation of breath he rolled away. Hearing him stand up, she smiled, stretched luxuriously with the satisfied conviction of someone who felt deeply adored. Lazily she opened her reluctant eyes.

She blinked. Instead of smiling down at her, he was heading for the door. There was something about his beautifully muscled back that told her he was controlling huge emotions. Ice froze her veins.

'Dimitri?' she whispered. A sudden panic took hold of her.

He jerked to a halt as if she had caught him with the tip of a whip. 'I didn't expect you to act the loving wife with such enthusiasm,' he muttered, his voice shaking and hoarse.

She felt as if he'd punched her in the stomach. But she fought her horror. He must never know how she felt.

'I've always enjoyed a healthy attitude to sex,' she flung recklessly.

'Perhaps that's why it's so enjoyable with you. No strings. Every man's dream. Have a shower. You know where to go.' And he slammed the door behind him with an unnerving finality.

CHAPTER FOUR

SHE felt desperately cold, even though the rays of the sun were streaming in through the huge picture windows and shimmering on her nakedness. Shaking uncontrollably, she snatched up her clothes, flushing with embarrassment to find them so thoroughly scattered about the room.

As she moved, she felt unsteady on her feet. At first she thought this was the after-effect of Dimitri's lovemaking. And then she discovered that the boat was moving and there was no sight of land.

Her head cleared as if it had been doused in water. Seething, she realised that the music must have drowned the sound of the purring engines and she'd been too overwhelmed by the glorious sensation of being loved to notice the gentle movement of the boat over the glass-like sea.

Loved! As if.

At the time, every instinct she possessed had assured her that he cared. But she had been wrong. It was just his technique. He'd taken what he'd wanted and then mocked her for her abandon.

A sharp pain of pure reality sliced into her chest. There would be no future for them. She had been fantasising. And she had misunderstood his eagerness. Of course he'd been seductive. Where women were concerned, he was driven by his loins. There had been no tenderness. Just sex. And she'd been conned. Bitterly she wondered how she could ever feel good about herself again.

Refusing even to think about what had happened, she held her clothes strategically around her body to hide her nakedness, and headed off to the nearest shower. She stayed there a long time, letting the relentless power of the water sluice her heated skin.

Her mind was in such a turmoil that she didn't know what to think. And so she blanked everything out, concentrating only on soaping herself with a punishing vigour.

'Olivia!'

She glared at Dimitri's abrupt call, thinking sourly that she wasn't ready for visitors. Hoping to drown out his knocking on the door, she turned the shower up to its most ferocious level.

'Leave me some privacy!' she yelled.

Her eyes were full of angry tears. She didn't want him to see her like this, vulnerable and humiliated.

The door opened, causing her to hastily get a grip on herself. It annoyed her intensely that Dimitri had walked in on her as if he had a right. But then he had always done exactly what he wanted and to hell with everyone else. Well, this time, she vowed grimly, she'd do the same.

Adjusting the bath sheet that was wrapped around his slim hips, he lowered his head and looked at her from under heavy brows. Silver droplets of water slid from his tousled hair and with an impatient hand he pushed his fingers over his scalp, smoothing his hair back to its normal sleekness.

Magnificent in his half-nakedness, he stepped into the spacious bathroom, his tanned body glistening with the sheen of water.

He looked composed, though his eyes were a hard black, like a slab of jet. The set of his mouth, the lift of his chest and shoulders, suggested that he was still struggling to master some tempestuous emotions. Nervously she wondered what they were. Triumph at seducing her? Scorn, disgust...

It was on the tip of her tongue to ask. Only pride stopped her. Avoiding his unnerving eyes in case she betrayed her misery, Olivia shut off the shower and grabbed the nearest towel, binding it around her body tightly.

'What's so urgent that can't wait till I'm dressed?' she snapped.

'I want to say that nothing has changed. I hold you to your promise,' he stated, a dangerous light in his narrowed eyes. 'With or without the sex.'

She gave a shrug of indifference as if the whole episode had been merely an indulgence on her part.

'I wouldn't like to embarrass you with my enthusiasm,' she said tartly.

'I'm not complaining. Enthuse as much as you like,' he growled.

'No thanks. I don't think I want to repeat that,' she clipped.

'It's of no importance,' he dismissed insultingly. 'Your promise is, however. Well?'

Thinking of spending two hours—let alone two weeks—with him made a quiver ripple through her glowing body, electrifying all the parts he had touched with such devastating results.

Whatever she claimed to the contrary, she knew that if they carried out this extraordinary plan of his they wouldn't be able to keep their hands off one another. There would be nights of unbelievable pleasure. Then would come the scouring emptiness that followed love-less sex.

Maybe she could live with that. She knew the score. He didn't love her.

To her eternal shame, she wanted him—with an all-consuming hunger that appalled her. Yet she didn't want the pain. Olivia bit her lip. The choice was stark: two weeks with him, or years spent fighting to be free of the chains that bound her to him like a prisoner to a stake.

And she had made a promise. She studied him. Arrogant, hard-jawed, implacable. A flare of anger surged through her. That was how he cut a swathe through the business world—and women.

Maybe he'd feel different if he was on the receiving end of such callous behaviour. Her eyes narrowed and she closed her heart to him. There was nothing wrong in enjoying sex with one's husband.

She would take what he had to offer—if she felt like it—and would bid him a cool farewell when her divorce came through. That would astonish him. His ego would be dented if she waved a cheerful goodbye. She smiled to herself.

Two weeks. She could do it because she needed him and hated him with equal passion. He was totally incapable of being faithful and she could never truly love a man who didn't put her at the centre of his universe. Whatever she felt for him, it wasn't love. Obsession, perhaps. Infatuation. But nothing deep and spiritual.

This was something she had to do, like an ordeal by fire. To sate herself with him until she was sick of him. Absence hadn't helped. Maybe this would.

Aware of his tension, she smiled and said casually, 'All right. I won't go back on my word.'

'So…we will be together.'

The vibrations of his deep tones raised goosebumps on her skin. 'Of course. We agreed to put up with the temporary discomfort as a means to an end, didn't we?' she said with a lift of her slender shoulders.

There was a long pause and he held her gaze while his eyes liquefied. He took a step towards her and she felt her heart slamming into her ribcage.

At that moment, the boat unexpectedly lurched forward and then back again. Losing her balance, she fell into Dimitri's arms. Although she tried to pull away, he held her tightly and after a moment she felt her flesh weaken and begin to flow into his. Quiescent, she looked up at him guardedly, allowing her body to respond—yet not her emotions.

'Yooo-hooh!' shrilled someone on deck. *'Ti yinete?'*

Dimitri froze. Olivia was wide-eyed at the sound of clattering feet. 'We've docked,' he explained hurriedly.

'But who—?' The words dried in her throat.

'Pedhi mou—'

Olivia recognised the voice at once. Purring the Greek equivalent of 'my boy', Dimitri's mother, flush-faced and excited, had come to the open doorway of the bathroom. Olivia swung around and Marina's elation turned to horror when she saw Dimitri apparently embracing his estranged, towel-clad wife.

'You!' Marina croaked.

Olivia blushed, her bare toes curling with embarrassment in the thick carpet. 'Yes. Me.' Her eyes narrowed, seeing the disappointment on Marina's face. 'You thought I was someone else. Who were you expecting to find?' she challenged.

It dawned on her that Marina's tone had initially been indulgent, almost frisky. She hadn't been surprised or horrified to see her son snuggling up to a semi-nude blonde. Perhaps, she thought darkly, Dimitri and Eleni's relationship had gone further than he'd said.

'Eleni! I—I thought it must be her!' Marina stammered, confirming Olivia's suspicions.

She tightened her mouth. Maybe Dimitri had already made Eleni his mistress, but drew the line at marriage with the girl. Rat!

'She has gone to meet her father,' Dimitri explained. 'Good afternoon, Mother. I'm sorry if we have embarrassed you. We weren't expecting anyone to drop in unannounced,' he added drily.

It was a mild rebuke, though affectionately spoken, and his mother's bean-thin body stiffened. Olivia felt sorry for her, though she remembered how her mother-in-law had frequently interrupted them, deliberately destroying their romantic picnics and quiet walks, intruding on their much-needed privacy.

'What's happening?' Marina quavered. 'Why is she here—?'

'I will tell you in private,' Dimitri said gently. 'It concerns the divorce. I'll meet you back at the house and we'll go into the details later. Olivia, I suggest you get dressed. You know where the bedrooms are.'

With that, he turned her around and gave her a light and playful husbandly slap on her rear.

Olivia whirled, intending to give him a piece of her mind in return, but he put a finger on her lips and sent her warning messages with his eyes.

'Remember your promise,' he whispered into her burning ear. 'And let me judge when it's best to tell Mother. She'll get the message soon enough.'

She glared at him suspiciously, wondering if he'd

stage-managed this moment. It was mighty convenient that his mother had walked in on them before they'd had the chance to get their clothes back on.

Their gazes clashed. His was amused and simmering with mischief; hers ignited immediately at the thought of turning the tables on him. A tingle spread through her body, setting it alight with excitement. She'd never felt so fired up.

Right, she thought, enjoying the challenge ahead. You want an adoring wife, then hang on to your hat. Because you'll get one with knobs on.

Languorously she wound her arms about his neck and kissed him on the mouth. She had one weapon. Her body. And she'd use it to good effect.

'Anything you say...*darling*,' she murmured, delighted when he shuddered and his eyes glazed over.

'Dimitri!' gasped Marina in alarm.

'Don't worry, Mother. She's a minx. I can handle her,' he murmured.

Flinging him a wonderfully warm and loving smile, she faced the woman who had helped to ruin her marriage. Marina seemed to be panic-stricken. Olivia's expression saddened. She pitied the woman. Marina would go through hell during the next two weeks or so.

'Please excuse me while I dry my hair and make myself presentable,' she said pleasantly. Her mouth quirked. 'See you in a moment, darling.'

Apparently cool and controlled, she patted Dimitri's bottom, gathered up her clothes and strolled past her bristling mother-in-law.

Dimitri watched Olivia's swaying body. Luscious. With the most clutchable rear he'd ever seen. A flawless back, her skin a glowing gold.

His entire body throbbed with memories of their lovemaking. She had quenched his passion in the most spectacular fashion. Dangerously, she'd come close to touching his emotions, but he'd remembered in time that she had used him—and was still using him to ease her own insatiable appetite.

'She's trying to win you back!' his mother declared anxiously.

He smiled at her in reassurance. Olivia had played the vamp for his mother's benefit with alarming sincerity. A woman who could lie so convincingly could never be trusted.

'I must dress,' he said with unusual gentleness. He went to her and held her stiff, bony body in a loving embrace. Then he kissed her cheek and pretended not to notice the tears which had sprung into her eyes. 'There's nothing to worry about, I promise. All will be well in the end. I have a scheme.' He saw his mother's face brighten. 'I'll see you at the house, as I said. We'll talk.'

'There's no time! I'm so busy! I planned a surprise party for you. It's all arranged for tonight,' she said in an unrecognisably small voice. 'To celebrate your coming divorce. You will be there, won't you?'

Dismayed, he knew he couldn't shame her by making her cancel it. 'Of course.' Tenderly he patted her hand. 'Thank you.'

Even in her expensive white designer dress and coiffed and tended by countless beauticians, his mother looked unsure of herself. It was as if she'd never been comfortable with wealth and might have been happier remaining a poor shepherd's wife.

He felt a strong sense of sympathy for her. His father had embraced the new life, working to build the business into the billion-dollar property empire it was now, with Angelaki developments springing up all over the world. But his mother had suffered from intense insecurity, terrified of doing and saying the wrong thing, unnerved by the social occasions she was expected to co-host. Gradually she had hidden behind a cold hauteur to disguise her lack of confidence and rarely let down her guard.

He wanted to find the laughing, tender mother he remembered from his childhood. The woman who had baked fat little bread men for him, who had run into the garden barefoot with him to watch sunsets. She was there—and he would find her.

He took her hand and kissed it with great tenderness. 'See you in a moment,' he said fondly and slipped into the stateroom to dress.

When Olivia emerged into the brilliant afternoon sun some twenty minutes later, she saw what she had surmised—that they had docked in the small fishing port of Olympos. Dimitri was leaning on the rail, lazily observing the sleepy little village whose cube-shaped houses clambered haphazardly up an olive-clad hill behind the harbour.

'Has your mother gone?' Olivia asked when she came to his side.

'Back to the house.'

'What did you tell her?'

'That you would be staying with us to keep our arguments as private as possible.'

'How did she take that?'

'Badly. I think she's afraid I'll find you irresistible,' he drawled.

She tilted her head insolently and put her lashes to good use. 'Maybe you will.'

His eyes caressed her and she surrendered to the delicious melting of her bones. 'I think we'll both enjoy our pretence. You know that's all it is, don't you?'

She snorted. 'I want to be free of you,' she said fervently.

Free of the compulsion to yield up her heart again. Free from having him constantly on her mind and in her dreams.

'Olivia...' Unusually, he seemed to be struggling for the right words.

'What?' she asked, frowning.

'I don't want to announce we're back together immediately. I want my mother to see for herself what is happening and to accept it willingly.'

'She won't! Not ever!' Olivia said fervently.

He frowned. 'You're wrong. She will if she thinks it's what I want. She accepted my marriage in the end—'

'No. You're wrong. She didn't.'

'That's ridiculous! I know what you think of her. You've told me often enough—'

'Everything I've told you is true,' Olivia said doggedly. Marina had been a bone of contention between them throughout their brief time together. 'You never believed me because she was always careful to keep her spiteful comments for when you were not around. But she undermined me and made my life miserable while you were away—'

He stopped her with an impatient wave of his hand. 'I'm not going over old ground. The past is past. Although she had reservations—and made them plain—she didn't say a word against you after our wedding day. Reading between the lines, it seemed to me that you made no effort to be friendly.'

'I did!' she insisted. 'I tried to fit in, to be a good daughter-in-law, but—oh, what's the use? It doesn't matter any more.'

'No, it doesn't,' he snapped. 'Except that I don't want to hurt her. She can't be unaware of the sexual chemistry between us, but our reunion is supposed to be something more. We need to convince everyone that we are falling in love. Understand?'

'Agreed,' she said quietly and, feeling a sudden flurry of nerves, she turned her attention to the scene before them.

'You think you can handle this?' he asked.

'It's worth it to get shot of you quickly. And there's the compensation of being here,' she whispered with a sigh of pleasure. There was nowhere like it on earth.

Fishermen mended bright orange nets, their heads bent low in concentration as their fingers flew in and out, deft and sure. The diamond-faceted water slapped gently against the streamlined sides of Dimitri's yacht. Children played happily on the nearby beach, their joyous voices ringing out excitedly.

She saw Dimitri's thoughtful gaze on the children and the spasm of pain that crossed his face at the same time that an echoing pain slid into her heart. How lovely it would be to have children to adore. Dark-eyed, dark-haired, strong and vigorous like Dimitri…

Impatiently she snapped out of her futile dream, wondering glumly if he still saw Athena and his child. The question burned inside her but she couldn't bring herself to ask. Instead, it sat like a cold stone in her heart.

'Shall we go?' she suggested, her tone hard with the effort of concealment. 'I'm looking forward to seeing the house again and swimming in that glorious pool.'

'I won't deny you the enjoyment of luxuries.' He looked disappointed, his eyes oddly dead as they walked to the gangplank. 'I'd better warn you that Mother has laid on a party at the house. A celebration of my divorce-to-be.'

'She doesn't waste much time,' she muttered. 'I'll hide in my room.'

'I want you there.'

'Your runaway wife? Won't people think that odd?'

'Unusually civilised, perhaps. But a public occasion will be ideal for our purpose. I have the impression that Eleni will be there.'

Olivia grimaced. 'How far do we go?' she asked.

'Lingering looks. Dancing too close. Too much touching,' he drawled.

She thought she could cope with that. Most of it would be for real, anyway. She just had to make sure she remembered that all his feelings were centred below his belt.

'OK,' she said airily.

'You have no problem with that?' he queried, clearly surprised she could contemplate being close to someone as compelling as him and not fall under his spell.

'Yes. One.' She produced a siren smile, her eyes dancing with amusement when he interpreted that as a tribute to his irresistible appeal. She simpered and sighed, 'I don't have a thing to wear!'

He laughed, but there was a challenge in his eyes. 'If only my problems were that small,' he observed in a drawl. 'However, all the clothes you left behind are still in your dressing room.'

'Are they? I'd have thought you would have flung them in the bin ages ago,' she said in surprise.

'The room was shut up the day you left,' he said abruptly. 'Come on. Let's go ashore.'

Olivia could hear the cheerful strains of lively music while she was trying on dress after dress, and discarding each one in a frenzy of indecision. Running to the window, she peered out at the pool terrace, where the party was to take place. White-coated waiters scurried about importantly among the classical statues and ancient urns, bearing silver salvers of food to a long buffet table. A small Greek orchestra gently switched from a traditional folk tune to a more sentimental ballad, a famous local singer huskily crooning passionate words of love and desire.

Marina hurried here and there, her thin frame resplendent in a long, glittering gown that must have cost Dimitri a fortune. This was a party to set him up for Eleni, she thought. How ruthless Marina was, to virtually sell her son to enhance her family standing with Greek aristocracy!

People began to arrive. Assured and elegant, they strolled around the pool, admiring the exotic plants and romantically lit statues.

Olivia's nerves grew worse. In despair she stared at the clothes heaped on the silk counterpane, uncertain whether to be demure and wifely or—as her instincts urged—to be a flamboyant temptress and thoroughly put Eleni's nose out of joint. It would be fun to explode on that scene. And, in the back of her mind, she knew she wanted to make Dimitri's tongue hang out.

'Not dressed?'

She whirled, flustered, glaring while Dimitri ran a raking glance up her stockinged legs to her lacy black suspender belt. He dwelt for a heat-seeking moment on her minimal briefs, then let his gaze wander up to settle on her breasts, uplifted by her balcony bra.

'Fantastic deduction,' she scathed when she'd got her breath back. 'Don't you ever knock?'

'It's my house.'

'But I'm not your woman!' she scowled.

'To all intents and purposes you are,' he pointed out.

She was trying not to look at him. One glance had been enough. Her heart had always fluttered when he wore a formal dinner suit and this was no exception.

The way his jacket had been moulded over his beautiful chest made her want to run the palms of her hands over his torso. His smoothly shaven face invited her touch or the pressure of her lips. Already she was aching for him. And they hadn't even begun their little play-acting for the evening. She groaned.

'This is a private room. I can throw things, you said so,' she muttered obstinately, contemplating a marble figurine with an air of menace.

'Throw whatever you like,' he said obligingly. 'But I must be seen to come in and out of your bedroom. Tongues must wag.'

'I suppose so,' she said grudgingly, and blindly reached for one of the dresses on the bed.

'Not that one.' He strode forward and took it from her hands. 'A nun could wear that and not be ashamed. This one.'

He held up the scarlet sheath she had longingly stroked and rejected without even trying it. This was her favourite—and had been his. But she hadn't dared to wear anything so blatant.

She wrinkled her nose in doubt. 'Isn't it a bit tarty?'

'Not at the price I paid,' he said. 'It's a knockout.

All eyes will be upon you. No one will be surprised when I spend most of the evening by your side.'

'Aren't you worried that Eleni and her father will be offended?'

'Everyone else will be willing us to get back together,' he said, holding the dress out for her. 'People are sentimental at heart. My business partner won't be able to show open disapproval, not when marriage is so important, so sacred.'

Sacred. Her lower lip quivered. If it was that special, why had he destroyed it?

'But your mother will go ballistic!'

'Not in public. And she will be consoled by the fact that the family will be spared the shame of divorce.'

'Until you reveal the truth and we really do end our marriage,' Olivia pointed out.

He smiled with infuriating self-belief. 'I'm confident that I can persuade her then that divorce is the only answer.'

'Oh, I'm sure she'll agree with you there,' she said wryly. 'She'll help you put the flags out.' Dimitri laughed, but she didn't. There was a sick sensation in her stomach. 'Two weeks. And then we'll both be free,' she mused.

'So let's make our bid for that freedom,' he purred, encouraging her to step into the dress. 'The sooner we start, the sooner we're rid of one another. Put this on.'

'I've only worn this dress once,' she said, hesitating.

'In New York,' he said throatily, his eyes glistening like melted chocolate. 'The Starlight Ball.' He smiled beguilingly, his gaze fixed on her parted lips. 'All those celebrities and you outshone them all. Everyone was talking about you. And I felt a hundred feet tall, having you on my arm.'

Her lashes dropped to hide her sadness. She'd been a bit of arm candy. An accessory to make him proud. And the bonus was that she was good in bed, too.

That decided it. She'd wear the dress and show him what he'd lost. One hell of a woman who'd loved him more than life itself. Who would have given him sons by the yard and daughters he could pet and adore. If only he hadn't been greedy and vain. If only he hadn't needed the flattery of other women.

The dress slid up her body, following her curves and hugging them possessively. On the pretext of smoothing creases, his hands shaped around the female swell of her hips and swept into the enticing dip of her waist.

He could hardly breathe. Obediently he responded when she turned her back, and slowly zipped up the dress. His fingers skimmed her warm buttocks and when he fastened the hook and eye almost at the base of her spine where the dress finished, he fumbled like a teenage kid who'd been offered his first chance to stroke a girl's nakedness.

'Let's see,' he growled.

Her eyes were bright and sparkling when she turned around again. He tried to cast an objective eye over her but it didn't come off. He knew he'd tensed. His teeth were jammed together, his loins were doing their own thing as usual and making him forget he had a brain at all.

At that moment, Olivia heaved in a breath, causing her incredibly high and generous breasts to swell alluringly above the low-cut neckline. He couldn't help himself. His head dipped and he was letting his lips move experimentally over them while his hands curved around her small and curvaceous rear.

She gave a little gasp and his mouth scalded hers.

He bent her backwards, revelling in her compliance, the silky material sliding sensuously over her willowy body. The pressure of her knee between his legs made him groan and intensify the pressure of his searching mouth as it travelled along the line of her jaw and then her pulsing throat.

Beneath his fingers the naked small of her back arched as she writhed against him, her arms dragging his head harder towards her in a satisfyingly fierce demand.

'Dimitri!' she whispered.

And brought him to his senses. He straightened, a mocking look in his eyes to hide his need.

'Isn't that proof enough? Your dress sets *me* on fire,' he commented tightly. 'Every man tonight will wonder why I don't put you over my shoulder and carry you off. Nobody will blame me for wanting you.'

'What a shallow lot,' she snapped, breathing heavily and adjusting her dress. He noticed the thrusting dark nipple of her left breast and wished he could surround it with his lips and tug it until she begged for mercy. But she had wriggled the scarlet silk back to its proper place and the moment was lost. She had seen his gaze, however. 'I'm just a body to you, aren't I?' she flung, hot and flustered. 'Nobody seems to care if I have a mind—'

'I did,' he objected, moving away and cooling himself down by standing at the open window. 'Once,' he added, before she got the wrong idea. 'Are you ready now?' he asked imperiously.

'Nearly.'

Her voice seemed to be shaking but he didn't turn around to see why. He needed a moment to steady his nerves. Many a time in the early days he'd been almost sick with apprehension before a big deal. But the way he felt now beat that hands down.

Tonight he must subdue his raw lust and dig out those long-forgotten gestures and glances of love that had been shut away in his heart. He knew that tapping into his emotions like that would be dangerous. Olivia had hurt him so badly that he'd vowed never to let any woman near his heart again.

He stared into the dark velvet night, inhaling the night scents. Behind him, Olivia fiddled with some jewellery. Perhaps she'd chosen the ruby necklace she'd left behind in the safe when she'd disappeared, and which he'd placed on the dressing table earlier, with the rest of the jewels that had escaped her voracious hands.

'Dimitri.' He stiffened against the softness of her voice.

'What?'

Olivia gulped. Her nerves were in shreds and he was barking at her! 'I need your opinion,' she managed, reasonably evenly. 'Tonight is important for both of us.'

With an irritable sigh, he moved from the window and faced her. For a moment his angry expression faded and she saw admiration in his eyes. Then the warmth vanished, to be replaced by coldness.

'You'll do.'

'Oh, thanks,' she muttered, slamming down the hairbrush.

His hands came down on her shoulders. They were burning hot, searing her skin as if he was branding her. In the mirror she saw his dark, enigmatic face close to hers.

She lifted her head in an unconscious effort to re-

main cool and detached and watched her pendant ear-
rings swaying gently, the rubies flashing in the centre
of the diamond star as if they were on fire.

'You look and smell wonderful. How much more
admiration do you want?' he grated.

She scowled, hating the way he treated her. When
he wanted sex he coaxed and purred. All other times
he walked all over her.

Huffily she replied, 'I only wanted to know if the
rubies were right—'

'They are. Time to go.'

Olivia felt like throttling him. But she'd get her revenge another way. Gracefully she rose and deliberately she lifted her narrow skirt to expose a generous
length of leg. Taking her time, and enjoying the fact
that Dimitri's breathing seemed all over the place, she
tucked her feet into a fabulous pair of jewelled sandals
before letting her skirt swish back to brush her ankle
bones.

'I'm ready,' she announced with a sweet smile.

It wasn't returned. Glowering, he muttered, 'I'll go
down first. Follow in ten minutes.'

'But—!'

'We can't arrive together. You need to make an entrance. I'm sure it will be a memorable one.' His assessing glance all but stripped her naked and the hunger
in his eyes made her stomach clench. 'I have no doubt
that we will leave together, however, and spend the
night inventively. You will surrender to me as you
never have before. And I will pleasure you until you
wonder if it is possible to die of that pleasure.' His
eyes blazed into hers. 'Keep that in mind all evening.
Think of it, anticipate it, hunger for it,' he murmured,
and was gone before she could draw breath from her
collapsed lungs.

CHAPTER FIVE

FROM her vantage point, with her shaking hands gripping the window sill, she watched Dimitri make *his* entrance down the broad flight of steps that led to the pool terrace.

Everyone seemed to stop talking for a moment. The women frankly stared. Men eyed Dimitri with open envy and admiration. He flashed a general smile at his guests and began to move among them, the genial and dazzling host she remembered from the parties they'd held here in the past.

Olivia saw Eleni detach herself from a group of giggling young women and head determinedly towards Dimitri, virtually pushing people aside in her eagerness to reach his side. He reeled under Eleni's enthusiastic hug, stepping sharply back so that Eleni's rapacious grasp was dislodged.

Enough was enough, she thought, loathing the way the girl simpered up at him. Now Eleni had begun to paw him on the pretext of admiring his jacket. Olivia felt as if her territory had been violated.

But she must remember that her role this evening was to *act* the swooning wife, not to *feel* it. And it annoyed her that she must seem to be besotted with him. It would flatter his ego too much.

Simmering still from Dimitri's searing promise, she told herself that his parting words had been part of the power game he meant to play. He wanted her passion to look real. She sighed. It might be. But she intended that his would also be real. It would be an evening *he'd* never forget. She had weapons too. And he'd go to bed frustrated.

Battle stations, she decided. Knots tied themselves in her stomach as she checked herself in the mirror. Would Athena be there with Dimitri's child? She couldn't bear it if she was. Though she imagined that since Marina had arranged the party, Athena wouldn't have been invited, not with Eleni taking centre stage. Was Athena still on the scene? She wished she knew— *needed* to know.

She heard the laughter below and bundles of nerves leapt and jiggled inside her. But this was too important. She couldn't let a few jitters hold her back from her purpose. The sooner Eleni had realised she wasn't likely to be Dimitri's next wife, the sooner she, Olivia, could escape Dimitri's clutches.

Brazen it out, she told herself. Enjoy rendering her arrogant husband helpless with desire for her! Tonight she was The Other Woman, despite being technically Dimitri's wife! She giggled.

Recklessly she teased her hair forward so that it curved seductively over one eye and she practised a sultry look. Laughing at the result, she took advantage of the fact that humour had eased her nerves a little, and sallied forth, every inch the seductress.

The walk down the marble steps was the longest she'd ever made. Her body ached from being held in tension as she gazed with apparent interest at the now silenced crowd and gingerly felt for each step with the backs of her ankles.

To her relief, Dimitri moved into the space at the bottom of the steps, his hand outstretched. The abandoned Eleni stared, wide-eyed.

She could have heard a pin drop.

'Olivia,' he said, as cool as cucumber and kissing her on both cheeks. 'Welcome.'

'Hello, darling,' she purred throatily, her arms curving around his neck so he couldn't escape. Her lashes batted flirtily. 'What a lovely party. I'm going to have such fun,' she purred.

His eyes twinkled. 'I can see that,' he said drily. With sheer force of strength he shifted to one side and broke her linked hands. She realised this was born of years of practice. There had probably been a whole list of women he'd grown tired of, and had given the brush-off to in the exact same way. 'Come and say hello to my mother,' he said forcefully, driving her relentlessly towards Marina's rigid figure.

Olivia swallowed and fixed a smile on her face as she dutifully kissed the cold, powdered face. 'Good evening, Marina,' she said, managing to keep the shake out of her voice. Marina was trembling and she felt pity for the woman. Dimitri had put them both in a very difficult situation. 'You look lovely, Marina,' she said truthfully. 'And I see you've arranged the party with your usual flair and efficiency. It all looks wonderful, and the lighting is just magical.' She admired the starry lamps, softly illuminating the scene, and the subtle floodlights which made the garden look mysterious and inviting.

'Thank you,' Marina said with a stiff inclination of her head. 'Do you know why I've thrown this party?'

'Yes,' she said brightly. 'To celebrate our forthcoming divorce. Such a good idea.'

Marina blinked, disconcerted by Olivia's level and uncritical tones. 'I...I didn't think you'd want to come,' she blustered.

'Dimitri insisted,' she replied with a smile, throwing the blame on him.

'I couldn't leave her in her room while we celebrated down here. It would offend my sense of Greek hospitality,' he explained with great gentleness. 'I'm sure everyone will think you are enormously tolerant and adult about my forthcoming divorce, Mother. They'll imagine you personally invited Olivia—and they'll applaud you for your generous spirit.'

Marina fluttered a little coyly and Olivia knew he'd made his mother feel better about the peculiar situation.

'I suppose it doesn't matter as Eleni is here.' Marina put her hand on Olivia's arm in an apparently confidential gesture. 'She and Dimitri have been very close over the past few months,' she whispered.

'Lovers, you mean?' Olivia said with a frankness that startled both Dimitri and his mother.

'Oh! I wouldn't know that!' Marina assured her archly, though it was clear she believed they were. 'But Dimitri has a man's needs—'

'Mother!' Dimitri said quickly. He was crushing Olivia's hand in his to stop her from bursting into laughter and she knew that he was controlling his laughter too. 'We mustn't keep you from your guests. And I think we should mingle, too. Excuse us.'

'A man's needs!' Olivia murmured when they'd moved off. 'You get carte blanche to do what you like, don't you?'

'Pretty well,' he agreed with a grin. 'And when I don't, I do what I like anyway.'

'No wonder you think the world turns around you.'

'Don't frown or they'll think we're having an argument. Smile sweetly and adore me,' he urged.

'*Pretend* to adore you,' she corrected, blinking stupidly at him till he lost control of his twitching mouth and broke into delighted laughter.

'What a night this is going to be!' he said cheerfully.

'*Evening.*' She didn't want him to be too sure of himself. It would give her pleasure to refuse his advances. 'Cinderella is leaving at midnight and Prince Charming will turn back into an ugly rat.'

His eyes twinkled. 'I said night and I meant night,' he murmured into her ear. 'And I think you've got the fairy tale a little muddled. Prince Charming was always the hero—'

'Not from where I'm standing. He has all the characteristics of a class-one rodent,' she shot, enjoying herself enormously.

'You can't accuse me of having cold blood,' he protested.

'A cold heart. And you scavenge for pickings from any heap of female flesh you come across—'

'Cinderella,' Dimitri said with a laugh, 'we have social duties. We'll continue this in bed.'

'We most certainly won't—!'

But he was already greeting his friends and she was forced to hold her tongue. 'Olivia,' he said with convincing warmth, 'I think you know several people here—but not, perhaps, my more recent business friends. My wife, Olivia.' She smiled at everyone a little nervously. 'She's here so we can arrange our divorce.'

There was a moment's shocked silence and then people began to introduce themselves. His easy-natured acceptance of her made it plain sailing after that. Clutching a glass of champagne, she found herself being directed from one goggle-eyed huddle of people to another.

During the ensuing conversations, she and Dimitri made sure they cheerfully explained their separate plans for the future—whilst flinging fond glances at one another. Olivia added the occasional flutter of her lashes, too.

She became aware that his hand was lingering on her naked back. That he was drawing her closer. And occasionally he seemed lost for words because he was staring at her as if hypnotised.

So she smiled up at him and let her widened-in-awe eyes do the talking. Her body was soon leaning in to his. It was like old times and it hurt, but she played along because she must.

Gradually she became bolder and flirted outrageously, reminding him constantly of things they'd done in the past. Although he seemed to be laughing with his friends at her witticisms and teasing, several times there was a warning light in his eyes. That only spurred her on to defy him.

'You have met my partner, Nikos Kaloyirou, before,' he murmured, whisking her away from a handful of people who'd been fascinated by the familiarity of their repartee.

Olivia sobered at once. This was Eleni's father, a distinguished-looking grey-haired man with pleasant features and a dark, assessing stare.

'Yes,' she said warmly as Nikos took her hand and kissed it gallantly. 'You came to London a couple of times when I was Dimitri's secretary. And of course you came to our wedding with your daughter, Eleni. But our paths didn't cross after that.'

Nikos nodded amiably. 'You probably know that I left immediately after with Eleni to set up the New York side of the business. We spend most of our time there now.' He lifted his glass in a silent toast. 'I remember how kind you were when I was in London and caught flu. You visited me every day, interrogated me as to my likes and dislikes and hobbies, and sought out books and magazines to amuse me. And you took my darling Eleni shopping.'

She'd forgotten that. The girl had been impossible: spoilt, rude and petulant, the vilest fifteen-year-old she'd ever known.

'It was fun,' she said, focusing on the attention she'd paid to the ailing Nikos at that time. 'I'll never forget the look on the newsagent's face when I walked off with a stack of fishing magazines, a book on fly-fishing and tying your own flies, a book on—'

'Dirty dealings while orchid hunting in South America and one particularly gruesome one on whaling in the eighteenth century!' Nikos finished with a chortle. 'I enjoyed your selection so much that I was almost sorry to be well again!'

During this exchange, Dimitri kept a smile on his face, but she knew he was uncomfortable and she wished they weren't deceiving this decent, honest man. She was about to make some excuse and leave when Eleni's raised voice made them all turn in surprise. She seemed to be berating a cowed waiter. Dimitri frowned and detached himself from Olivia, till Nikos stayed him with his hand.

'My dear daughter has such passions!' he said fondly. 'She'd give you a good run for your money, Dimitri!'

'I'm sure she would,' he agreed.

Nikos grinned, winked at Dimitri meaningfully and strode off to placate his daughter.

'He adores her,' she commented.

'And is blind to her bad habits.'

'Does he know you sleep with her?' Olivia dared to ask.

Dimitri choked. 'That's the second time you've accused me of that! What gave you such a stupid idea?' he spluttered.

'Things,' she muttered with a vague wave of her hand. 'You said she was physically stunning. Since that's all that registers with you where women are concerned, I assumed—'

'Smile,' he murmured. 'Your claws are showing.'

She pinned on a particularly soppy expression and he laughed, annoyingly dropping a kiss on her nose.

'You didn't confirm or deny your relationship with Eleni,' she persisted.

'I don't have to. The only thing you need to know is that I don't want to offend Nikos. And that I am determined not to be hustled into marriage. I especially need to beat it into Eleni's head, and my mother's, that I am not interested in nineteen-year-old girls who have temper tantrums. Like that,' he added grimly.

For a moment they watched the red-faced Eleni stamping her foot while her father ineffectively remonstrated with her.

Olivia chuckled. 'I almost feel sorry for you,' she said with a grin. 'If I were truly vindictive, I might consider leaving you to Eleni's mercy.'

'Mercy?' he said ruefully. 'She'd have me committing suicide in a week.'

'Rubbish. You love life far too much for that. Come on.' She wrapped her arm around his waist, feeling extraordinarily cheerful. There was something wonderfully abandoned about being The Other Woman! 'Let's do a bit more play-acting. *Darling.*'

'Wicked witch,' he muttered, and nibbled her ear.

Olivia allowed her shudder of delight to surface, knowing that they were being watched and that people near by were leaning in their direction to listen to their conversation.

'Naughty.' She retaliated with a little nose play of her own, tapping him there with her forefinger. His eyes gleamed and she giggled as she continued, 'What will your divorce lawyer say to such behaviour?'

'Right at this moment, I don't care,' he growled sexily. 'Tonight you are my wife and I intend to claim my rights.'

He pulled her roughly into his body and she only just kept her head, remembering that this was all make-believe. So she lifted an arched eyebrow and purred seductively, 'Ohhh! I *love* it when you're so dominating, like some puffed-up little potentate!'

His mouth twitched at the dubious compliment. And he whispered in her ear, 'Watch it. You might regret that remark by breakfast time.'

'Sounds thrilling,' she said, eyes sparkling with devilry.

'It will be. I promise.'

She laughed in delight and dragged him a short distance to four of his male friends who'd been riveted by their banter. They were all over her like a rash and seemed to find it almost impossible to unglue their eyes from her cleavage.

Dimitri played it to the hilt and became even more possessive. She loved every minute of his growling attention, and several times found herself gazing up at him with real adoration when she forgot that he was only pretending to be jealous.

He was appalled at the ease with which she flirted.

Years of practice, he supposed. And in between she was managing to look at him with such melting love in her eyes that it made him want to shake her till she begged for mercy. Now he knew how she'd deceived him in the years up to their marriage. Even her eyes could lie convincingly.

'Tell me, Olivia,' said his friend Vangelis, his voice flatteringly croaky. 'Will you stay in Greece after the divorce?'

'You'll be very welcome,' butted in a bemused Andros, addressing her bosom. 'Especially in my house.'

'All of me or any particular part?' she asked with a grin, and Dimitri's irritation was swapped briefly for a smile.

'Oh, all, yes!' Andros said fervently. Dimitri worried cynically for his friend's blood pressure.

'That's very kind,' she murmured with a sweet smile. 'Thank you.'

'Time we circulated,' Dimitri growled, and the men all looked at his menacing face warily. 'I'd better tell you that Olivia is less certain about her future now we've met up again. And I'm becoming more and more uncertain about mine.' He let his gaze rest on Olivia, staring deeply into her eyes.

'Does that mean…you two…?' Vangelis left the rest in mid-air.

Dimitri's hand stroked her shoulder and she looked up at him with naked adoration, before fluttering her lashes and adopting a more flirtatious glance.

Lying eyes. Lying little tease! he thought, barely controlling his anger. He touched her parted lips with his forefinger, cynically admiring her clever little gasp that had his friends completely fooled.

'Can't comment now. Watch this space,' he said in a parting shot, and whisked her away to a quiet, unobserved corner.

It would have given him the greatest pleasure to put her over his knee and slap her tight little rear. Hell. Why was he so jealous?

'I knew you'd make an impact,' he muttered tightly through his plastered-on grin, 'but I hadn't expected my intellectual friends to mislay their brain cells quite so comprehensively.'

'That's the trouble with men and breasts sometimes,' she said perkily. 'The face doesn't get a look-in. All normal communication is diverted southwards.'

'You encouraged them,' he growled.

'I was only doing what we agreed,' she defended.

'And so very well,' he mocked. 'But it didn't include making eyes at everything in trousers.'

'It's good for people to see that you can be jealous,' she said, suspiciously demure.

He caught hold of her impatiently. 'I just don't like men thinking you're up for grabs. You're still my wife. Behave with some decorum and don't bring your London morals here.'

'Is this for real, or are you merely *staging* a show of Jealous Husband Syndrome?' she asked, her eyes wide with wonder in the semi-darkness.

And he realised he was in danger of betraying the fact that he was behaving 'for real'. So he conjured up a thin smile and tried to make his eyes join in.

'Me? Jealous? If I wanted you, I could have you. There'd be no competition in sight. It would all melt away.'

Her hand stroked his cheek. 'Such unbelievable conceit,' she sighed. 'And so misguided.'

'Like hell it is!'

Provoked to the limit, he kissed her. Hard at first, then softening his mouth as hers began to yield. When he released her, he saw that her eyes were unnaturally bright.

'What an exhibition we're making of ourselves,' she commented, desperate to hide her misery. Her mouth burned. Her heart felt sore. But she'd never let him know what he did to her.

'I think my intention is clear,' he rasped. Placing his hand on her rear, he added, 'Isn't it?'

'Painfully so. Is mine?' she countered sweetly.

And she risked a saucy wriggle against him before she squeezed his hard, neat rear too, while she kissed him back, pulling away when he tried to prolong contact with her lips.

He looked annoyed. 'Crystal. It seems we have the same goal in mind,' he growled.

No, she thought. Yours is domination and bed. Mine is escape from a ridiculously obsessive relationship that's destroying me.

'This'll be interesting,' he said, before she could come up with a quip. 'Eleni's heading this way. Think you can deal with her on your own?'

'Coward,' she chided.

'With good reason. I'm trying to prevent two inches of pancake make-up from being plastered all over my dinner jacket,' he grunted.

'Well, you disappear, then,' she said, giving him a push. She didn't want Eleni slithering all over him either.

He hesitated. 'I think,' he said hurriedly as Eleni bore down on them, 'it would be a good idea if we catch each other's eyes across the crowded terrace a couple of times. OK?'

Olivia nodded and held her hands out obediently, ready to 'catch' his eyes. Always quick on the uptake, Dimitri laughed, kissed her cheek and slipped away just as Eleni barged past her last obstacle—two teenagers ogling Dimitri as if they wanted to eat him whole.

'Hello, Eleni,' Olivia said cheerfully, getting in first. 'It's ages since we met. I remember taking you shopping—'

'I was a kid then. It was before I got these.' Eleni defiantly thrust out her shiny breasts at the startled Olivia. 'I must say, you've got a nerve, flirting with Dimitri! Don't you know he's mine? He is my *lover*. So don't muscle in or I'll scratch your eyes out.'

Lovers. Who was telling the truth—Eleni or Dimitri? After all Dimitri's lying in the past she'd rather take Eleni's word. It seemed that Dimitri would take sex in any form, even when he despised the woman involved.

Olivia winced. Dimitri despised *her* and yet he wanted to make love to her. Maybe he felt like that about all women.

Soberly Olivia gazed at Eleni. The girl seemed very confident, but when Olivia looked more closely she saw that beneath the glamorous make-up was a very young and possibly insecure young woman. Studying the sullen, resentful face, Olivia decided that she couldn't blame Eleni for adoring Dimitri. He'd turn any woman's head.

So she smiled with some sympathy, making no reference to Eleni being Dimitri's mistress. Even if the jealousy scoured a hot well of anger inside her.

'It's three years since Dimitri and I were last

together,' she said evenly. 'We're having fun, reminiscing.'

'Is that what you call it?'

Olivia shrugged. 'It's amusing to tease him. Too many people treat him like some kind of god. He needs bringing down to earth.'

'You can do that without draping yourself all over him!' Eleni protested. Olivia dared not comment. 'How long are you staying?' Eleni asked bluntly.

'As long as it takes to get the divorce.'

'In that case, why are you making eyes at him? You don't love him!' Eleni blurted out. 'You never loved him!'

She looked at Eleni sadly, every raw wound suddenly exposed. 'He was my life, once. My soul mate...'

Something made the hairs on her neck tingle. Something compelled her to turn. And when she did, her gaze honed in on Dimitri like a heat-seeking missile. He was staring at her, and the impact of his impassioned eyes made her draw in her breath and she found herself walking in his direction as if propelled by an unseen force.

Remembering her manners, she flung back confusedly over her shoulder, 'Excuse me.'

Eleni was looking at her in astonishment, blinking at Olivia's dry-throated whisper.

'I must go. You see how it is,' Olivia breathed.

And she glided away, seeing that Dimitri was striding purposefully towards the garden, politely but briefly replying to comments from the guests he passed whilst constantly checking that she knew where he was going.

Around her she could hear the buzz of conversation increase in volume and she knew they were talking about them both, about the strange powers that drew them together.

But this was what they'd planned. A very public recognition that the sparks hadn't died in their marriage. It was also very true.

Stooping to remove her shoes, she padded over the billiard-table lawn to Dimitri, feeling as if her body flowed towards him with the same inevitability as a river flowing to the sea.

Her eyes were almost midnight-blue when she looked up at him. He gave a shudder, his longing apparent in every inch of his tensioned muscles.

'I want to make love to you, here and now,' he muttered, his voice riven with passion. 'I want to see your limbs spread on the grass, your arms reaching up for me.'

She shivered, rivulets of pleasure rippling through her pliable body. 'A rather extreme way of indicating to everyone that we're getting back together,' she croaked.

His head inclined and he gave a wry smile. 'My conclusion too. Unfortunately.'

He sounded rawly husky, as if he too had trouble with a desert-dry throat. Olivia felt weak. They'd always have this incredible chemistry between them. Nothing, no one, could ever affect her as deeply as Dimitri did. So she blurted out the first thing that came into her head.

'I—I had to get away. It...seemed a good idea to wander over here,' she said, her eyes huge in the darkness at the telling of the little white lie. But she couldn't let Dimitri know that he had caught her in his web as a spider caught a fly and rendered it helpless.

So she babbled on. 'I thought Eleni might throw her drink over me and I didn't want my dress ruined.'

Her heart began to pound when his arm lifted and he reached out to lightly stroke her hip. 'No. It would be a shame. It suits you so well,' he said jerkily. Retracting his hand and thrusting it deep in his pocket, he frowned and cleared his throat. 'I'm afraid she regards me as her property.'

The atmosphere thickened between them as if the air was being filled with silent messages they dared not speak. She swallowed, trying to keep the thread of the conversation in her dazed mind. Yes. Eleni. Her eyes flashed.

'With good reason.'

'Nobody owns me,' he growled.

'No. But some people have rights where you're concerned,' she said sharply.

It was appalling that he thought he could treat his mistresses with such contempt. First Athena, then Eleni. And goodness knew how many in between.

'Was she being bitchy?' he asked, ignoring her comment.

'It wasn't a conversation I wanted to continue,' she admitted.

Dimitri sucked in a long breath and let it out slowly. 'I know she's difficult but she's had a strange upbringing. Her mother died when she was tiny. A series of nannies have spoilt her,' he said gently. 'And it can't help that Mother gave her the impression this was *her* chance to shine and yet everyone's talking about *you*.'

'Oh!' she said, flustered, her face flushed from the compliment. 'I don't think so—'

'I can assure you they are. They're all bowled over

by your beauty, your poise and your easy manner. I
am constantly being told what a fool I am.'

She went pinker still, reluctantly but undeniably
weakened by the throbbing richness of his low tone.

'I'm not surprised they're gossiping about us,' she
said, attempting levity. 'It's not often a man entertains
his wife and his wife-in-waiting at the same party.'

He chuckled. 'With any luck the wife-in-waiting will
become the one that got away.'

'She'll be devastated.' Olivia frowned, worried for
the girl. She'd lost her virginity to a monster. 'You
shouldn't have slept with her,' she reproved.

'How many times do I have to tell you? I haven't!'
His scowl suggested that her accusation offended him.

'That's not what she says!' she persisted.

'Then she's lying. Wishful thinking. I swear it. She
has a crush on me, nothing more, and she was trying
to warn you off. I'm far too old for her,' he replied,
and she felt certain he was sincere. Her spirits lifted.
Maybe he wasn't such a heel after all. 'There are several young men of her age who are more than eager to
step into my shoes and they'll suit her much better.
She won't have to pretend to be sophisticated and she
can take off those layers of make-up and be her nice,
natural self. It's buried there somewhere.'

'I hope you're right. I don't like hurting people,' she
said slowly.

'Really?'

Her lashes flicked up at the note of disbelief in his
voice. 'I make an exception with you,' she muttered.

His grin slashed the darkness. 'I thought so. Now,
to scandalise everyone a little more and to get the sen-
timentalists sighing, I suggest we walk up and down in
full view,' he directed. 'Take my arm and talk to me.'

They strolled through the garden, lit by huge, gut-tering candles. Its beauty tugged at her heartstrings and added to the turmoil of emotions that threatened her judgement. She felt as if she might suffocate with the tension that hung around them and prevented her from breathing normally.

Aching with the effort of walking without stumbling, she was glad when they paused to look out at the lights of Olympos village twinkling in the darkness and the necklace of lamps edging the waterfront. Tantalising perfumes teased her nostrils as they drifted in on the breeze. She could smell lemon blossom and it was so sharp and poignant that she began to tremble from the memories it evoked.

'I want to go back to the party,' she said, weak-kneed, weak-willed and frantic to go before she said something she'd regret. Like *I love you and I always will*.

'You can leave any time,' he murmured, as if he understood the reason for her sudden distress. 'I'm sure people here have got the message about us.'

The gentle expression on his face tore into her heart. In a moment of madness she reached up and drew his head down, kissing him tenderly. Then she pulled away abruptly before she confessed her true feelings.

'In case they haven't, I hope that does the trick,' she croaked out with as much brightness as she could man-age, and hurried back to the fascinated throng as if she was escaping from a dangerous animal. Which she was, she thought wryly.

'What exactly are you up to?' snapped Eleni, ac-costing her with angry belligerence.

'I've no idea,' she blurted out honestly. 'I wish I did.'

Blindly skirting the crowd, *en route* to goodness-knew-where, she was halfway across the empty dance floor when Dimitri caught her up.

'Dance with me,' he said in a tone that brooked no refusal.

Not that she wanted to refuse. She was in his arms and swaying to his every movement before her brain could warn her against such a silly move. And she was loving it. Her head nestled in the hollow of his throat. His breath seared her scalp hotly. The glory of his body lured her in until her curves lay against his, her breasts leaping into sharp peaks where they were rubbing the soft wool of his jacket. The burning pillar that heated her pelvis grew harder and harder and his grip on her hand grew tighter as their breathing shortened.

'Look at me!' he whispered in hoarse command.

Helplessly she did so. He stopped in the middle of the floor. Took her face between his hands and looked at her for what seemed an eternity, her eyes swimming under his impassioned gaze, before he swept her into his arms again and continued the dance, even closer than before.

This couldn't go on. It was beginning to hurt, the pain of loving him tearing at her heart so fiercely that she almost cried out loud.

'Wait,' Olivia ground out when they were level with the small orchestra. She managed to push herself free and begged the bandleader for something lively.

Dimitri laughed when she returned to him. 'Can't stand the heat?' he murmured.

'Can't stand being pawed. Darling,' she whispered, plastering a sweet smile on her face.

'Like a bit of action, instead?' he drawled and, catching her by the waist, he whirled her around the floor till she was breathless.

Despite her reluctance, she began to enjoy the hectic excitement of dancing with a man who knew how to lead, whose movements she could anticipate so well that it seemed the two of them had rehearsed for hours. And it was a release for her pent-up emotions.

Soon the dance floor was empty and they were working through their repertoire of energetic jive-cum-rock and roll, to suit the rumbustuous music.

Bright-eyed, laughing and exhausted, they finished with an exhibition twirl that evoked a storm of applause. Dimitri looked down at her flushed face, his heart thundering.

He'd forgotten what it was like to feel like this. To have his heart and mind dominated by something other than luxury apartments and executive houses. She made his bones sing. Little witch. But it was a great feeling and he meant to string it out as long as he could. He was enjoying himself too much to let her leave Greece quickly—though he needed to stay in control. She must dance to his tune, not the other way round. That meant he had to call a halt now.

'I must dance with my mother,' he said with private reluctance, wanting to hold Olivia in his arms all evening.

Her luscious mouth parted in a pout. 'In that case, I'll share myself around too,' she sighed.

His grip tightened before he could help it. 'Not too enthusiastically,' he muttered. And hastily added in harsh warning, 'You're supposed to be falling in love with me.'

'Oh, I'll fling you plenty of soppy glances,' she said, patting him like a pet dog.

With gritted teeth that made his jaw ache, he watched her closely for the rest of the evening. It seemed to him that she was having more fun than she should. His friends had claimed her, one after the other, holding her tightly to their chests and gazing down at her with stupefied expressions.

Propping up the bar, he glowered to see her lapping up the admiration. Eleni was hanging on his arm, chattering away. Every now and then he nodded or made a comment on her inane babbling.

But his mind was elsewhere, captured and tied up in ropes by a stunningly beautiful woman who lit fires in his veins, whose supple swaying body had been burnt on the backs of his retinas so that wherever he looked he could see her, and wherever he was he could hear her musical voice and flirty little laugh.

'Dimitri! You're not listening to me!' Eleni shook his arm crossly.

'Sorry.' He dragged his brain back. 'What were you saying?'

'It doesn't matter. You're hooked on her, aren't you? And she's a bitch, deliberately trying to make you jealous. Can't you see that?' sulked Eleni.

There was pain in the girl's eyes. Tenderly he took her hands in his. 'Olivia and I—'

'Her flirting is deliberate! She knows I'm a rival!' she said with a sniff.

'Eleni!' he said in consternation.

Olivia was nibbling canapés at the huge, flower-garlanded buffet table on the terrace when she caught sight of Eleni disappearing into the house. Closely followed by Dimitri.

Her stomach contracted in horror and she slid her

plate onto the table, her hands shaking. He couldn't. Wouldn't. He'd sworn they weren't lovers. Yet the way he hurried after his partner's daughter—as though he was eager to catch her up and kiss her and sweep her into his arms—suggested otherwise.

She would find out. Perhaps expose him for the liar that he was. With a mumbled excuse to Andros, she made her way up a set of side steps to the house.

Where she found Eleni wrapped in Dimitri's arms.

CHAPTER SIX

QUIETLY she slipped away before she was seen, her heart thundering in her chest and her mind teeming with confused thoughts. How could she be so stupid as to love such a man and give her heart and soul to him so comprehensibly? He'd never been true to her. Had never been honest.

And the stupid thing was that she'd *known* they were playing a game. He'd made it plain that she was just a body that he'd virtually hired to rid himself of an unwanted bride-to-be. Yet she realised now to her intense shame that unconsciously she'd harboured wild, crazy hopes that maybe...*maybe*...

She'd been incredibly gullible. Dimitri only had to murmur a few lying sweet nothings and she was his. She ought to have known better. Past experience should have told her that all he wanted was sex without strings from any willing, beautiful woman who happened to be around.

Sure, he found her desirable. But, she thought miserably, he thought loads of other women were desirable too. Whatever had given her the impression that she might be someone special?

Huddled against a marble pillar on the upper terrace, she morosely surveyed the glittering scene. Then with a sigh she glanced down at her fabulous dress. Right now, she'd gladly swap all the glamour here for a little house and a man she could love, who respected her and was utterly faithful.

Wearily, sick of it all, she found another door into the mansion and stumbled to her bedroom. Remembering Dimitri's promise of a night of passion, she jammed a chair beneath the handle on the bedroom door.

He could make do with Eleni, she thought, violently unzipping her dress and slinging it in the direction of a chair. It missed and fell to the floor, but she let it lie there, hoping sourly that Eleni would spend the entire night giggling into Dimitri's ear and numbing his brain with inanities.

Too tired to think, she prepared for bed mechanically and eventually slipped on her black silk nightdress and crawled into the soft linen sheets with a sigh of relief. But as she lay there, longing for sleep, her mind began to replay the evening in full Technicolor.

There was Dimitri, dark, handsome, apparently adoring. There he was again, laughing. The whiteness of his teeth and the amusement on his face caused her body to tighten even now. He seemed to be everywhere in her head. Deceptively loving. Painfully good-looking and desirable.

She put her hands to her head, desperate to be rid of him. With a groan, she sprang up and poured herself a glass of wine from the carafe by the bed, thinking that a good slug of alcohol might make her drowsy. It didn't.

Muttering angrily under her breath, she paced the room, and even tried counting backwards from a thousand. Somewhere around nine hundred and thirty she lost the plot and found herself quivering at the memory of Dimitri's touch.

It was going to be a long night. Resigned, she

stomped over to the window to glare at the few remaining guests. No Eleni in sight.

Surprisingly, Marina was still up, dancing with Nikos. Olivia wondered if her mother-in-law might be a little drunk, because she seemed to be melting in her partner's arms, her gaunt face so remarkably relaxed and happy that she looked quite pleasant for a change.

Olivia tensed. Dimitri was there, too, chatting amiably with a handful of friends in that easy, male style. Her eyes softened. He sat in a wicker chair, every inch the Greek tycoon, his arms draped casually over the arms, one long leg crossed over the other. And he looked immaculate as ever and totally unperturbed, as if he hadn't spent the past hour or so smooching with a nineteen-year-old girl.

Suddenly he stiffened and glanced up at her window, as if he'd known she'd been staring at him. Olivia hastily moved away, upset that he'd seen her. With his giant ego, she thought crossly, he'd probably think she was mooning over him like a lovesick fool, while she'd been mentally firing lasers at his steel-clad heart.

Dimitri's head reeled. There had been an uncharacteristic droop of her shoulders that warned him something wasn't quite right. The narrow straps of her nightdress had been slipping down her arms. In fact, her whole demeanour had been strangely listless. Despite the distance between them, he was sure her mouth had been set in an unhappy line. He had to go to her. He didn't know why, only that he must.

Using well-honed tact and skill, he managed to persuade the last guests to leave. Stifling his impatience, he thanked the orchestra and the caterers, then hugged his mother, who hadn't said a word about his extraordinary behaviour throughout the evening—presumably because, as he'd guessed, she dared not object in public that it looked as if his marriage might be saved.

'Don't worry about me. Everything's under control,' he said, anxious to put her mind at rest.

'I won't,' she said before he could continue. She smiled with unusual warmth at Nikos, who had brought two brandies over. 'I know you're up to something. Besides, I've decided that I have my own life to lead and you must make your own mistakes.'

Astonished, Dimitri looked from one to the other, noting the new softness of his mother's face. Nikos gave him a sheepish look and a helpless shrug. A little dazed, Dimitri said his goodnights and left them to it.

All he had on his mind was Olivia. In truth, she had drowned out almost everything else all evening. Racing up the stairs, he tried to open her door. And found it wouldn't budge more than an inch.

'Olivia!' he called. 'It's me.'

'I hardly thought it might be anyone else!' she shouted back crossly.

He frowned. 'Let me in, then.'

'If you think I'm entertaining you after you've been canoodling with another woman, you're sadly mistaken!' she yelled.

What was she talking about? Irritated, he pushed the door again and it yielded slightly.

'Open this door or I'll break it down!' he ordered.

'You've been watching too many American movies!' she retorted. 'Go back to your lover and leave me alone!'

He had no choice. Refusing to discuss her wild accusation through two inches of oak, he took a few steps back, steadied himself, and charged, thinking to shock her into opening the door. However, there was a re-sounding crack as something gave way and he was hurtling into the bedroom.

'Get out of here!' she cried, shocked.

Cringeing against the bed hangings and clinging on to them for dear life, she looked so terrified that he calmed down immediately. He kicked aside the broken chair which had allowed him entry, then pushed the door shut and leaned against it, trying to look harmless.

'So—other than you—who am I supposed to have made advances to tonight?' he asked in amusement, loosening his bow-tie and undoing the top button of his shirt.

'Good grief! Don't you know?' she hurled.

'No. And I think I would have noticed,' he pointed out with a grin.

'It's not funny! Allow me to jog your memory,' she seethed. 'Curvy blonde. Spectacular body. Giggles a lot.'

'*Eleni?!*' He laughed at the very idea. 'Heaven help me, I've told you before—she'd be the last woman on earth I'd approach.' His eyes twinkled. 'How could I fondle a woman whose breasts are solid marble?'

'How do you know they are?' she demanded hotly.

'I don't,' he replied with great patience. 'I'm assuming they would be since they don't move a lot.' He looked pointedly at hers, which were moving more than he could personally withstand.

'You don't deny you've looked, then?'

He heaved a sigh. 'It's difficult to escape them when they're sitting like cannonballs on top of her dress. Olivia, I keep telling you. I'm not interested in her—'

'Then it was her double who I saw in the salon in your arms—'

'Ahh. That's it.'

'You're not denying it now, are you?' she flung, sounding at the end of her tether.

She was truly jealous. For some reason that delighted him. Vanity? No. Something else that he dared not investigate.

'Olivia.' His voice and his entire demeanour softened. 'Eleni *was* in my arms. But, as I recall, we were fully dressed and we remained clothed throughout the time I comforted her.'

'Oh, yes?' she muttered sulkily.

'I saw that she was upset,' he explained. 'I decided to enlist her as an ally.'

'That's ridiculous! You're lying to me,' she accused.

'Not at all. I am aware that she needs people to think well of her. Therefore I remarked on the fact that she and I had always been good friends and that I knew she would want the best for me. I said she'd always seemed like a kid sister to me—'

'Bet she hated that.'

'It made her blink,' he agreed with a wry smile. 'And while she was temporarily speechless I managed to talk at length about marriage being a sacred union between a man and a woman—'

'What a liar you are!' Olivia glared.

'And,' he persevered, 'I got her to agree with me on the sanctity of marriage. She'd realised what I was doing by then, but she could hardly say that it meant nothing.'

'Devious.'

'I thought so,' he said, pleased. 'I told her I was entrusting her with a secret and that you and I were getting back together. She burst into tears and I said I knew how sentimental she was and how kind of her to feel so happy for me that she felt like crying. I imagine that's when you saw us, because almost immediately she pulled away and wiped her eyes before stomping off to dance with Vangelis.'

He willed her to believe him. But he didn't tell her what else he'd said to Eleni.

'You...didn't...do anything else? Like...kiss her?' Olivia asked in a small voice.

He winced at the very idea. What would convince her? 'I swear I didn't, on my father's head,' he said simply.

There was no arguing with that. Dimitri would never use his father to support a lie. She bit her lip, cursing herself for jumping to conclusions. Dimitri had been acting kindly to Eleni by letting her down gently.

'I'm sorry,' she mumbled.

'It was an understandable mistake.'

'Yes, it was, considering your reputation!' she muttered.

'And what reputation is that?' he asked mildly.

'As a womaniser.'

'Ah.'

No denial, she noticed. 'You're pretty untrustworthy where women are concerned.'

'Am I?'

She glared. 'Don't tell me you've been celibate ever since we parted!'

'No. I haven't.'

She flinched at his honesty, wondering how many, how often, how beautiful those women had been.

'I suppose I should be pleased,' she said jerkily, 'that you have persuaded Eleni to abandon her hopes of marrying you. We can bring this awful charade to a close...'

She gulped. Why was she appalled at the thought of a rapid divorce? She ought to be celebrating, but it felt as if she were at a wake. Turning away to stare sightlessly out of the window, she tried to control her swamping misery.

Dimitri's hands rested lightly on her bare arms and she felt a jolt of lightning flash through her.

'And we can be free to do whatever we want,' he finished for her.

All she wanted was to love him. To trust him. To be the only woman in his life. Some chance.

When he tried to turn her around she resisted and escaped, backing away, her eyes wide with apprehension.

'Well, I want you to leave,' she said in a low voice.

'No, you don't.'

His sheer arrogance made her eyes flash with instant defiance. When he smiled, and took a step towards her, she picked up the half-full glass of wine and hurled the contents at him.

'I do!' she cried, as most of the wine fell to the floor.

Unperturbed, he shed his wine-stained jacket and shirt, letting them drop in a heap.

'That is a lie,' he said calmly.

Alarmed by the determination in his glittering black eyes, she grabbed the carafe and began to eject its contents at him, backing nervously as he advanced on her. Wine gleamed darkly on his chest, trickling over its planes into little valleys and wetting the dark hairs that curled in a dark, tapering line that led towards his loins.

'I'm going to make you lick all that up,' he growled, unhooking his belt.

'Dimitri…no!' she croaked, dazed by the thought of sliding her tongue around the hard contours, and teas-

ing each tight, male nipple into an erection... Her hand
went to her mouth and she blushed, finding that the tip
of her tongue had already moistened her lips as if in
eager preparation.

'Could be a glorious way of getting tipsy,' he
breathed.

It was the way he looked at her that sent electric
thrills pulsing into every nerve of her body. She could
feel her flesh softening beneath the sensual impact of
those wicked black eyes, which were heating her like
blazing coals till a furnace burned inside her.

'Why should I want to do that?' she demanded,
clinging by a thread to normality.

'To throw off those peculiar inhibitions you seem to
have acquired since I last made love to you. Put down
the decanter, Olivia. It's cut glass and will cause damage to those bare feet of yours if it smashes. Those
beautiful feet... I wouldn't want them scarred.'

The hunger was eating away at her, unfairly reminding her of long-ago pleasures. Dimitri, taking each foot
in turn and exploring every inch with his mouth.
Sucking her toes while watching her with blazing hot
eyes.

Shakily, she put the decanter on a marble table.

'This isn't what I had in mind!' she whispered.

'Isn't it?'

Somehow she shook her head instead of letting herself drift into his arms. 'No. You said we'd pretend to
be crazy about one another in *public*. Well, no one is
here to see. We can behave normally—'

'I am.' He spread his hands in innocence.

She glared. 'I'm sure that's true. You'd come on
strong to any woman who looked vaguely willing—'

'Not at all. I'm very fussy,' he purred. 'I only like

women who make my body quicken with a mere glance. Who are so aware of their sensuality that it characterises every movement they make. Who can abandon themselves to the possession of their senses and lure a man on till he thinks he's going crazy. Women who respond to my touch. Who shiver and shudder and love bodily contact—'

'Don't!' she whispered, aghast at what he was doing to her.

He was talking about *women*. How many did he know who'd given him such exquisite pleasure? And…how had he got so close to her? She hadn't noticed him moving. Only the dark promise in his velvety eyes. She took a step back and found that the wall was touching her spine. Trapped. She had only her wits left to keep him at bay—and they seemed hell-bent on deserting her.

'Go and find one of those women, then,' she scorned, tossing up her head with a defiant swirl of her hair. 'I'm only here as a means to an end—our *divorce*! I'm willing to continue the farce of gazing at you idiotically in public, but don't get any ideas that I'm game for a little light sex in private—'

'It won't be little and it won't be light.'

The soft murmur ran through her like a hot wave that melted where it touched. His mouth curled in anticipation and she found herself unwillingly watching its sensual curve. Her breath shortened and she almost leaned forward to kiss those amused lips, wanting to shut him up, to impose herself on him and to remind him that he could be *her* slave when it came to sex. Because she didn't want him to seek out another woman. She wanted him for herself. Exclusively.

An impossible dream and she knew it. 'You have to leave!' she jerked out.

He smiled, as unconvinced by her breathless order as she was. 'It seems such a waste when you're here, those gorgeous summer-sky eyes sending me enticing messages I can't ignore—'

'They're telling you to go!' she cried, but lowered her lashes, knowing they were doing nothing of the sort. And her gaze hovered again over his intensely masculine mouth. The urge to drive her lips into his and kiss away all her tension was overpowering.

'Olivia, be honest,' he murmured as her hands screwed into tight fists. 'Admit what you feel. I see it in every line of your body. The way you tremble. The swelling of your lips. The thrust of your nipples, forcing against the black silk so hard that I can hardly keep my hands from touching them. You don't know how difficult it's been for me, trying to get you to own up to your feelings instead of ripping off those straps and letting your nightie fall to the floor so I can see and touch and claim your body.' He paused, his voice husky. 'We are virtually free agents. We can do what we want,' he whispered. 'And at this moment I want *you* with every beat of my heart.'

She gasped with fury, his near-seduction ending as if he'd dropped her into cold water. 'At this *moment*?' she spluttered. 'Oh, thanks! I'm pleased to be considered for your diversion *at this moment*. And who might you want at any other moment? Like this afternoon, tonight, tomorrow? How *dare* you! I'm not someone to be picked up and put down as the fancy takes you! Maybe you didn't want to spend the night with Eleni sniggering in your ear, but that doesn't mean you can turn to me for your sexual comforts just because there's no one else suitable around!'

She had never looked more beautiful, with her eyes sparkling, mouth parted and ready for his kiss, her head flung back and that lovely neck exposed. He had never wanted her more. Or been so determined to have her.

'I'm not treating you as a poor substitute for anyone,' he said, croaky with need. 'I have spent the entire evening waiting for this moment.'

His hand reached out, surprising him by the way it shook. Quickly he let it rest on her moon-silvered shoulder, then slowly slid it to linger on that slender, silken throat. She gave a little gasp, which emboldened him to move closer. His other hand slid into her perfumed hair till he could feel the warm curve of her head.

'The love between us might have died,' he said quietly, 'but the sexual attraction is hotter than ever. Isn't it?'

She didn't reply, but gazed at him in consternation. It was agreement enough for him. But he wanted her to say it. So he leaned forward a little and lightly touched her lips with his. He felt her breath heating his mouth in fast, jerky little bursts.

'Isn't it?' he persisted, tasting her with the tip of his tongue.

Her eyes closed, seemingly in despair. After a long, breathless moment, she whispered with a moan, 'Yes!'

The silk slithered down her body in an agonisingly erotic movement. He felt an odd little stab in his chest. Standing there, naked and glorious, she seemed vulnerable. Beaten.

'Olivia!' He took her in his arms and held her close. At first she remained stiff and tense, yet trembling like a leaf. But because he did no more than hold her she slowly relaxed. And when she lifted her head and looked at him he saw something of the old Olivia, a passionate and proud woman who rejoiced in the extraordinary chemistry between them.

And then her mobile rang.

Dimitri groaned. 'Leave it,' he muttered, kissing her throat.

'No... ' She drew in a sharp breath as his teeth nibbled her lobe. When he began to suck it, she pulled away and snatched up her bag. Sitting on the bed, she avoided Dimitri's eyes and dragged the duvet over her nakedness.

This was her chance to cool down. To give her brain an airing instead of letting it sink like a stone beneath her appalling lust.

'Hello?' She cringed at her quavering, froggy voice.

'Olivia?' Paul sounded puzzled.

'Oh, yes!' she said brightly. 'Paul! How *lovely* to hear from you.' Dimitri sat on the bed, much too close to her. Covering the mouthpiece, she flung him a false smile. 'It's Paul,' she said unnecessarily, then, crushed by Dimitri's mocking eyes, she jerked her head away and attended to what the lawyer was saying.

'...fabulous time. Angelaki has an entire skyscraper for his company alone. We've got a brilliant settlement—'

'But—'

'You'll be free of him pretty soon,' Paul hurtled on. 'And a multimillionairess! How about that? Don't you think I've done well?'

'Paul, I—' She slapped Dimitri's hand away. It had slid beneath the duvet and was slinking its way up her leg.

'It's OK. Don't thank me. I'm hoping you'll come over to New York,' Paul said smugly. 'I've some fantastic news! Guess what, Olivia!'

She grabbed the corner of the duvet, which Dimitri was tugging free. Glaring at him, she snapped an irritated, 'What?' into the phone.

'Are you all right?' Paul asked, just as Dimitri flung his weight across Olivia and bore her back to the bed. 'It's not too late, is it? I tried to work out the time difference, but frankly I'm in such a whirl that I'm not sure—'

'I'm fine,' she gritted, fending off Dimitri's determined assault on her bared thigh. His hand was smoothing it with an infuriating rhythm and she seemed to be getting short of breath as her need began to dull her brain.

'Good. Well, this is my news,' crowed Paul.

'Oh, help!' she whispered, feeling herself surrendering to the passionate kisses being rained on her jaw and throat.

'I,' Paul announced proudly, 'have been offered a job by the Angelaki New York office.'

'A...job?' she said, incredulous. The news was like an ice-cold shower. Stiff and resisting, she glared at Dimitri, who was openly listening to the conversation while kissing the line of her jaw.

'That's right. And you know what American lawyers can earn! This is my chance, Olivia! And—well, I don't need to tell you this because I know you and I had a kind of understanding—together we could be a great team—'

'Paul,' Dimitri murmured, having snatched the phone from her, 'take the job and be grateful. You're not having Olivia as well. Is he, my darling?'

'Give that back!' she gritted, struggling. Dimitri grinned at her. His body effectively held her a prisoner and she couldn't reach the phone.

'One more thing,' Dimitri said, his tone edged with steel. 'Learn the time differences if you want to keep your job. It's the early hours of the morning here and we're in bed.'

'Bed?' she heard Paul screech.

'Luckily we weren't asleep—if you know what I mean,' Dimitri drawled, then disconnected the call and flung the mobile on the floor. 'Now, where were we?' he mused. 'Here? Or here—?'

She jerked her head to one side and he just managed to avoid kissing the pillow. 'Don't *touch* me!' she breathed in fury.

His hand cradled her cheek and he pushed firmly till she was forced to face him again. His eyes had darkened dangerously.

'Is your conscience troubling you?' he muttered. 'That's the little voice in your head, by the way, that tells you it's not decent to chat to an ex-lover on the phone while your husband is about to ravish you.'

She ground her teeth together. 'Why did you instruct your people to give Paul a job?' she demanded furiously. 'I know you have an ulterior motive in doing so—'

'Correct. I'm ensuring he's off the scene.' Dimitri's mouth came down hard on hers in a long kiss that left her gasping for breath. 'It was obvious to me what he had in mind. He wants to marry you and I can't allow that.'

'Why?' she defied, as if she might contemplate the idea.

'Because he's not man enough for the job.'

'And you are?'

His eyes gleamed. 'Definitely. I intend to remind you of that. Right *now*.'

CHAPTER SEVEN

THE sun was gently turning her body a golden brown. She knew she ought to turn over to do her back but she didn't have the energy…thanks to Dimitri.

With a slow and languid lift of her arm, she tipped back her floppy sun hat to observe him. He, too, had been utterly still for the past hour, stretched out on one of the steamer chairs beside the pool.

The effort of holding up her hat was too much and she let it drop. But she could still see him in her mind. There was a warm glow inside her when she thought of his hard, toned body gleaming in the sun. His arms hung limply to the ground as if he was exhausted, too. Dimitri's sensual mouth seemed at odds with his strong, masculine profile and she wondered if he was thinking of the hours they had spent in bed—and out of it—till mid-morning.

Faint quivers trickled deliciously in the channels of her limp body and seeped into her very bones but she was too sated to be aroused.

It seemed as if time had been suspended. The air hummed with the heat, a slight breeze bringing tantalising scents to her nose. A stillness had descended on the garden, broken only by the gentle swish of the palms surrounding the pool.

She heard the maid, Maria, offering lemonade. The sound of it being poured and the clink of ice.

'Olivia,' murmured Dimitri.

A cold glass touched her fingers that draped negli-

gently on the hot tile and she gave just a drowsy
'mmm' of thanks. Her hand was grasped, kissed, then
released. She heard him returning to the lounger and
settling himself with a contented sigh. As well he
might.

She loved him. Not because of the unbelievable,
earth-shattering sex, though that would have made any
woman feel she'd found paradise on earth, but because
they had talked and laughed too, and she had felt truly
happy, utterly at ease with him.

All the feelings she'd had for him in those heady,
early days when they'd first begun to work together
were back in force, but far stronger now.

Dimitri had caressed her and loved her until she'd
thought she might die of pleasure, and even at this
moment a little sigh was escaping from her kiss-
swollen lips at the very memory of those hours of bliss.
But for her the sex was a part of something greater that
involved her deepest emotions. He was more than a
drug—he was essential to her happiness.

The thought filled her with alarm. She sat up
abruptly and sipped the cold drink, hoping to steady
her wild thoughts. Because if that was true then she
had to fight for him. To make him love her more than
he loved his freedom to enjoy other women. And how
could she ever do that?

Dimitri reached out lazily, his hand touching her
arm. 'I will never forget last night,' he said huskily.

'Nor will I.'

She hesitated, tempted to pour out her feelings, to
take the risk that he'd laugh and say it was great but
not for keeps. But the familiar voice of Eleni trilled out
behind them and she groaned and clamped her lips together instead.

'Did I drive all thoughts of Paul from your head?' he probed.

'Yes—'

'Dimitri!' Wearing a crop top and brief skirt over a bikini, Eleni flung her arms about his neck and virtually sprawled over his body. Olivia groaned. 'Lovely party, darling,' she purred, toying with the lock of hair that had fallen onto his forehead. And she began to murmur under her breath to Dimitri.

'Get off, wretched child!' he complained.

Olivia put down her drink and went for a swim, even though she was too tired to do much more than drift about aimlessly in the silken blue water, floating on her back with her eyes shut against the sun.

After a moment, two splashes at the far end of the pool told her that Dimitri and Eleni had joined her. She lifted her head to watch. They were fooling about, ducking one another as if they were the greatest of friends. No, she thought, seeing how often Eleni managed to slide her body against Dimitri's. More like prospective lovers taking every opportunity to touch.

Tears stung her eyes. Every time she thought Dimitri really cared, she discovered that it was merely part of his seduction technique. If he did care, he wouldn't fool about with Eleni.

She turned and began to swim to the edge but suddenly she found herself being grabbed and pulled under water. She kicked out and emerged spluttering to see Eleni's laughing face a few inches away.

'Got you!' Eleni crowed.

'You certainly did,' Olivia said without amusement.

'Jealous?' Eleni taunted.

She looked for Dimitri. He'd disappeared. 'Should I be?'

'Oh, yes. I'm Greek and his partner's daughter. And I accept that the men of my country are passionate and have many affairs.'

Olivia blinked in astonishment. 'You'd let him have affairs?'

'Sure. If it meant he'd stay married to me. It's rumoured that his father had a mistress. I'd have to accept that Dimitri would probably have one too.'

Olivia knew that Dimitri had idolised his father. When Theo had died she had spent hours talking to Dimitri and comforting him. After he'd returned to England from the funeral she had done everything possible to ease his grief. A week later he had proposed.

Perhaps, she mused, it had been a mistake to marry on the back of tragedy. Maybe Dimitri had needed emotional support after losing the father he loved, and had thought marriage would provide that. It wasn't a good enough basis for a long and stable relationship, though.

One thing she did know: if his beloved father had maintained a mistress then Dimitri would have accepted that as the norm. It wouldn't be surprising if he believed that fidelity wasn't important—at least, not where he was concerned. Her spine felt as if a cube of ice were sliding down it.

'I don't know how you could contemplate sharing him,' she said soberly.

Eleni shrugged. 'Better that than nothing, so long as it's discreet. Though if he upsets me once we're married, or if he harms one hair of my head, my father will see to it that the Angelaki empire collapses.'

Olivia was appalled by the girl's ruthlessness. Eleni had set her sights on Dimitri and wouldn't be put off.

'Personally,' she said quietly, 'I'd rather have the

devotion of a man because he adores me, not because he's been threatened with financial ruin.'

Olivia swam away and climbed out of the pool. The girl had been spoilt and given everything she wanted. Eleni might idolise Dimitri, and imagine that being married to him would be all roses, but she didn't love him. Love was more than sexual attraction and starry-eyed dreams.

Thoughtfully she rubbed her hair dry with a towel. Love weathered all difficulties. It grew... Pausing in her reverie, she smiled at the masses of geraniums in a terracotta urn near by. Grew like a flower. She'd been madly in love with Dimitri from the moment she saw him. The seeds of passion had been there already, but she had grown to love him more profoundly as time went on.

Her heart thudded painfully. Perhaps she was giving up too easily. At least Eleni was fighting for the man she wanted.

Maybe it was worth the risk of being hurt. She could try persuading Dimitri that a deep and loving commitment to one person was infinitely more satisfying than casual affairs. Slowly she dabbed at her damp skin, trying to decide whether to follow her heart or her head. Her brow furrowed. Was she thinking like a woman, and forgetting that men felt entirely differently?

From inside the house, he watched Olivia tensely, knowing she was chewing over something that troubled her because she'd been drying the same part of her firm little rear for the past few minutes.

With difficulty, he dragged his mind from those tempting curves, irritated with himself for being so easily distracted. But her body was gorgeous, the sun gleaming on it lovingly, and he couldn't help but relive his recent exploration of every squirming inch.

He slapped his hand against his forehead in rueful exasperation. Olivia invaded his mind so thoroughly that sometimes he wondered if every brain cell he possessed had her image emblazoned there.

His greedy gaze enjoyed the rhythmic movement of her hands, a stab of remembered sweet agony slicing through him. She could drive him crazy with those delicate, wicked fingers. With her wholehearted, utterly abandoned responses to his touch.

She was biting her lip and frowning. He hoped she wasn't worrying about Eleni's behaviour. That girl needed a firm hand. If he hadn't left the pool when he did, he knew she would have done something outrageous and he would have been forced to slap her down—with disastrous consequences. He knew how vindictive Eleni could be.

His tension softened at the sight of the pensive Olivia. Their odd sense of psychic communication ensured that her head lifted and she saw him watching her. She gave a little gasp, then, flinging down the towel in a determined way, she tied a colourful wrap around her body and walked towards the salon, where he stood, still in his swimming trunks.

He smiled, anticipating the kiss they would share. As she approached, he opened the double doors that led to the terrace.

'Your little chat with Eleni didn't work. She intends to marry you,' she said bluntly, stepping past him into the room so quickly that her hair whisked over his bare shoulder.

He made the quivers die down in his body, but the

scent of her remained to provoke him. Here were the memories of last night, of the morning, crowding in on him, rendering him weak with desire.

'I know.' He cleared his throat of the huskiness that betrayed him. 'She told me so a few moments ago and I tried to laugh it off—without success, it seems.' His eyes gleamed with slumberous pleasure. 'We must try harder to convince her that we're back together again and she doesn't have a chance.'

Olivia frowned and the tip of her small pink tongue touched her lips. 'Yes. Or I'll never... ' She bit her lip this time. 'Never get the divorce, will I?' she finished rather shakily.

He sensed a reluctance in her, which suited his purpose very well. If he played his cards right he could spin this out till he was rid of his addiction to her. A year, maybe. Studying her huge blue eyes and the thick fringe of lashes, he felt a thrill start its journey through his body.

Her face assumed an expression of drowsy longing. He began to plan a day of unrestricted lovemaking, his gaze wandering avidly over her curves, outlined by the clinging wrap. And she gave a little gasp, her breath shortening like his.

'Olivia!' he whispered, managing just a croak.

'Yes?' she mouthed, and he felt compelled to move forward, to seal her hot lips with his in a long and thorough kiss.

His hand drifted into her hair. He tipped up her chin and smiled, shaking with overwhelming feelings for her. Sexual, of course. Nothing more. He'd sealed off his heart three years ago and she was the last person he'd allow to break that seal. But she made every cell in his body leap with life and he wasn't intending to let her go till he'd exhausted his passion for her.

'More passion,' he ordered thickly.

'What?' Her voice shook very satisfactorily.

'Eleni is watching,' he whispered, and took her mouth in his, crushing it in an explosive kiss that had her whimpering in need. 'Convince her!'

'Yes!' she moaned.

Dizzy with love, she writhed hungrily against him, finding joy in being in his arms. For a moment she could pretend that he cared. She knew she was taking a risk with her emotions but she couldn't help it. If there was a chance that Dimitri might recognise how well they were suited, then he might learn to love her.

She lifted a long bare leg and slid it down his thigh. He gave a shudder and beneath her palm she felt the acceleration of his heart.

'It's good, isn't it?' she whispered.

He groaned, hating her, wanting her. His mouth savaged her throat as she sighed and pressed her warmth against him; he felt his skin scorch where her naked flesh met his.

He had to tell her. She must agree to stay. The uncertainty was gnawing at him till he thought he'd go mad.

'You know it is. You know that you drive me crazy,' he muttered.

'Do I?' she murmured with a languid smile. Her sharp teeth nibbled at his lower lip.

He pulled her deeper into the room, out of sight, and took her head in his hands to focus her attention on what he was saying. 'I don't want you to go,' he said hoarsely. 'Stay with me.'

She gasped. 'Dimitri—' she whispered.

'Stay.'

He saw her eyes fill with tears. The radiance of her face made his stomach clench. This was what she'd wanted, he thought helplessly. She thought she'd got him back for good. But it was only till he'd had enough. The mother of his children would never be a gold-digging tramp.

'For...how long?' she asked, her tear-washed eyes searching his.

He hauled in a shaky breath and kissed her, losing himself in the taste of her mouth, the feel, the smell of her.

'I don't know,' he said honestly.

'I'm afraid.'

He frowned, his finger idly brushing back and forth across her nipple. 'Of what?'

'Being... ' A faint moan fluttered from her parted lips. She moved his finger to her other breast and began to breathe hard when its peak surged into life beneath his rhythmic touch. 'Being sh-aa-red,' she jerked.

'Listen to me.'

He looked down at her closed eyes, the soft lashes thick and luxurious on her beautiful cheekbones. Her head was thrown back, her mouth moist from his kiss. He would do anything, promise anything to make her stay. Night and day he thought of her. Some time he had to drag his brain back to work, but while she possessed it so utterly he was useless.

So he stepped back. Held her at arm's length. 'Olivia,' he said, 'I wouldn't be interested in other women if we were lovers again. I'm not that much of a stud!' he added with a smile, and was curiously flattered when she seemed to doubt that. 'You take everything I have to give and leave me sated—until you look at me with those hungry sapphire eyes and then I want to devour you whole. There will be no other women. You have my promise.'

'Not...even a brief fling with...with any of the women you've been involved with since I left?' she asked in a small, anxious voice.

His face cleared. 'Absolutely not!' He laughed. 'They were a disappointment. I'm afraid I compared them with you and found them wanting.'

'No one...special?' she probed, concern in every line of her face.

He pulled her into his arms. 'No. You will be the only one. I swear on my father's head. Please stay.' And he waited, holding his breath while she stared at him, perhaps making up her mind, perhaps keeping him dangling. He didn't know, didn't care, only that she should say yes.

She held her breath. It was worth trying. She must put the past aside and think of their future. Maybe she was gambling with her happiness, but she'd never forgive herself if she didn't make the attempt.

When she smiled, hope leapt in his chest. Her smile widened and lit her eyes till they gleamed like jewels.

'Yes,' she murmured, and a strange delirium hurtled through him.

Steady, he warned himself. But her palm lovingly shaped the contours of his chest and her mouth sucked delicately at his nipple. The familiar wildness came over him. Olivia would be his and his alone. Exulting, he lifted her head and drove his mouth hard on hers while his fingers slid to the tie of her bikini. Her hand closed over his.

'Not here. Not with Eleni hovering in the background. I want us to go somewhere,' she murmured, flushed and bright-eyed. 'Somewhere romantic.'

He smiled and showered kisses on her face. 'I know just the place,' he breathed. 'I'll tell her we're leaving. Get dressed and collect what you need. We'll take a trip out in the boat away from here, away from Eleni and Mother. Just you and me, enjoying ourselves.' His hungry mouth nibbled her warm shoulder. 'The bonus is that it'll look good, the two of us sneaking off together.'

It sounded wonderful. And perhaps it would be her opportunity to show him how much she loved him. They'd spend the day together, just as they used to. She wanted to remind him how comfortable they had been with one another. If she could revive that sense of belonging, of deep conviction that they had always been destined for one another, then he might realise what he would lose if he ever risked playing the field.

Her dreamy smile made her face radiant with happiness. It was quite possible that they might be together for ever, she thought. And let out a long, satisfied sigh.

'I'd like that very much, Dimitri,' she murmured. Winding her arms about his neck, she eyed him with open adoration and was rewarded by his indrawn breath. Her forefinger touched his mouth and he gently savaged it with his teeth. They would talk. Make love. Forget everything but the future. 'Somewhere private,' she whispered. 'Where we can swim and...sunbathe.' Closing her eyes, she let her soft lips close on his.

Briefly she felt the flicker of his tongue, and then he was gently unpicking her fingers. 'Go,' he said thickly. 'I can't wait.'

She shuddered, running an exploratory finger over his biceps and down his arm, her eyes holding his in a long, loving look. 'I'll be ten minutes,' she whispered, joy lighting her face.

Hand in hand, they strolled to the harbour. She wore a simple sky-blue top with bootlace straps and a matching skirt that swirled about her legs. Dimitri looked edible in a cream open-necked shirt and chinos.

Joyfully she joined Dimitri in greeting the black-garbed women with merry eyes that they passed, and the wrinkled old men who drowsed in the sun on rickety chairs outside tiny cafés dripping with bougainvillaea.

'*Kronia pola,*' she said happily. Many years.

'*Epsis,*' they replied. And the same to you.

Olivia thought of the many years she might spend with Dimitri and couldn't stop smiling.

Her senses seemed acute. She could smell garlic and lemon, and the sound of sizzling came from the small taverna on the quayside.

Her heart seemed to expand. This was where she wanted to be. This was the man she wanted to share the rest of her life with. Providing he committed himself to her.

A tremor of uncertainty collapsed her confidence, but when she looked up at him and he smiled down at her, squeezing her hand affectionately, she remembered his oath and told herself she was being unnecessarily neurotic.

In companionable silence they clambered on board his small motor launch, and Olivia stood with her arm around Dimitri's waist while he eased a passage between the sturdy fishing boats.

'Where are we going?' she asked, enjoying the wind whipping her hair back from her face.

He gazed down at her with heart-jerking affection. 'Wait and see.'

Snuggled up to him, she felt his back muscles expand as he manoeuvred the boat around the rocks scattered like broken beads at the tip of the island before heading out to the deeps, the breeding ground for sharks.

After a while they passed the volcanic island of Methana and seemed set for Poros Island. Slipping through the narrow channel between Poros and the mainland, they began to hug the coast. And Olivia knew where they were headed.

She couldn't stop smiling. He had remembered.

He drew the boat up on a small sandy beach and lifted her out as if she were a new bride crossing the threshold of the marital home. Symbolic, she thought, her heart catching with happiness.

Setting her down gently, he collected the small rucksack he'd brought and took her hand.

'I can smell the lemon blossom,' she said softly.

He smiled. 'I thought it would be a good place for a picnic.'

'Perfect,' she sighed as they left the beach and began to walk through a field of poppies, starred with white daisies. Flowers bloomed everywhere, as they did in Greece: in the ruined walls of some long-forgotten temple, in rock crevices, and—exuberantly flooding the area with a tapestry of colour—beneath the trees in the lemon grove.

'Fabulous.' Drenched in the heady scent of the lemon blossom, she could hardly speak for joy.

They sat on a low hill with views down to the lapis-lazuli sea, their backs to a warm wall where tiny lizards basked. Olivia put her head on Dimitri's shoulder and they remained in awed silence for a long time, their arms around each other.

It was so peaceful they might have been the only people in the world. Olivia thought dreamily that he *was* the only person in the world for her. And it was enough just to be with him, her troubled mind calm at last.

'Look. Swallowtails.'

She followed Dimitri's pointing finger and saw the butterflies hovering over the rock roses and sage. Now she could see little blue butterflies too, flitting about the wild lavender and rosemary bushes which were dotted about the lower ground.

Drugged by the lemon blossom, choked with happiness, she let her gaze wander over the orchids, fritillaries, anemones and blazing, blowsy poppies.

'I thought of this place so many times when I was in England,' she said quietly.

He kissed her, the first of many kisses that day. They kissed and touched and hugged one another often, and it seemed to her that he too was in a hazy dream.

Lazily they ate their simple meal of olive rolls with herbs, cold *kleftedes*, cheese, and cinnamon doughnuts soaked in honey syrup. Dimitri licked the syrup from her fingers and her lips, then fed her cherries and sweet oranges. They stayed in the grove for a long time, sipping wine and talking.

'You said you were between jobs. I hope you didn't have a male boss in the last one,' he muttered.

Olivia laughed and her expression told him that she was intent on teasing. 'I *did*. But he was seventy-one and could never catch me when I ran around his desk!' Dimitri glowered and gently sank his teeth into her bare shoulder. 'I'm fooling,' she said. 'He finally retired and his son took over. I didn't like the way he looked at me or the comments he made—as if he fancied his chances—so I gave in my notice. And that's when I decided it was a good opportunity to call you and say I wanted a divorce.'

Dimitri stared out to sea, his heart thumping. A tiny suspicion formed in his mind. 'So you don't have a job now.'

'No. Which means I can stay.'

He was silent. Had she planned this all along? Handed in her resignation and deliberately set out to ensnare him again?

She began to kiss the side of his face and after a moment he turned his head back to her, his eyes shuttered.

'Fortunate,' he rasped, and pushed her back to the ground.

She felt dizzy from the perfume around them, the wine, his searching, demanding mouth. Her arms wound around his neck and she lured him with her eyes.

'Let's go for a swim.' He had pulled her to her feet before she could comment.

But she loved him, so she indulged him. They stripped and walked into the sea, which was as warm as a bath. She was too sleepy to do much more than float or tread water, but Dimitri powered his way up and down the little bay as if his life depended on it. Amused, she waited till he emerged, water sluicing from his body, and slowly joined him on the beach.

They dried one another and she felt such love for him that she thought her heart would crack. They walked to the headland to watch the sun set. As the crimson sky turned to a dusky black, the cicadas began to whirr in a deafening chorus. Fireflies speckled the darkness as they wandered back to the launch.

Olivia curled up on the sumptuous leather cushions, weak with rapture. He hadn't even made love to her. Sex had been superseded by something deeper: the delight they shared in being together. Sighing, she flung her head back and stared at the deep velvet sky and its pinpoints of tiny stars. She wanted this to be her destiny. And yearned for it to be permanent.

CHAPTER EIGHT

SLEEPILY, aware of the morning light, she flung a loving arm to Dimitri's side of the bed. Her eyes shot open. Her hand had landed on an empty space. She listened for the sound of the shower, but all was silent, except for the low murmur of voices below on the terrace.

Curious, she slid naked from the bed, her body still humming from Dimitri's tender lovemaking.

He was having breakfast with his mother, drinking *sketo*, the unsweetened coffee he favoured, and talking to her earnestly. Olivia smiled, guessing that he was giving his mother the news that their marriage had been saved.

Yawning, she stumbled to the shower and pulled on a pair of briefs and a simple white sundress, pleased with the golden tan she'd acquired the day before. Pausing only to put a pair of pearl studs in her ears, she fiddled impatiently with their fixings before hurrying down to the terrace.

'Olivia!'

Dimitri leapt to his feet when she appeared and came to kiss her cheek.

'Hello, darling!' she beamed. 'Hello, Marina.' She bent to kiss her mother-in-law. 'How are you?' she said, taking the chair Dimitri held for her.

'Very well,' smiled Marina vaguely, making Olivia blink with surprise. And then she discovered the reason for Marina's rather distracted manner. Nikos appeared, greeting them all—but with his steady gaze lovingly fixed on Marina.

Dimitri and Olivia exchanged amused glances. Nikos had stayed the night. And in whose bed? they signalled to one another.

'Nikos,' Dimitri said quietly, 'I want you to be one of the first to know. Olivia and I are back together again. I hope you are pleased. I know how you feel about wedding vows.'

He looked shocked for a moment, then his inbred courtesy came to the rescue. 'Of course. Congratulations,' he said a little stiffly.

'I imagine you'll be organising Eleni's wedding soon,' Dimitri went on tactfully. 'There are so many men buzzing about her I think she's spoilt for choice.'

Nikos gave a grin of pride, his disappointment eased. 'She's a catch.'

His eyes strayed to Marina, and Olivia wondered if Nikos would beat his daughter to the altar. She began to relax, feeling like the cat who'd got the cream, and tucked into her breakfast of yoghurt, fruit and honey with enthusiasm while Marina and Nikos chatted like children on a spree.

'I don't think they even noticed us going,' she giggled, when she and Dimitri stole away.

'Mother's a different person,' he said softly. 'Being in love changes everything.'

'Yes,' she agreed. 'It does.'

And she waited for him to make some kind of declaration to her. Or even to suggest they found another romantic spot—where he could tell her how deeply he was committed to her. Pulses fluttering, she waited in vain and bit her lip to conceal her disappointment.

They had reached the hall and he had remained silent, engrossed in thought. At that moment she heard his mobile ring. She automatically stiffened, her heart sinking at the familiar and much hated sound. Many times in the past that wretched tune had heralded a change of plan, and she didn't want that to happen this time, not when so much should be said about their future together.

'Shan't be a moment.' He glanced at the read-out and stiffened. 'Go up. I'll be with you in a moment.' Preoccupied, he gave her face a casual caress then pushed open his study door and slipped inside.

As she turned away despondently she felt her earring slip to her shoulder and then fall to the ground, its weak fastening probably dislodged by the brush of Dimitri's hand. On her knees in search of it, she found herself staring into the study past the half-open door. Her stomach wrenched at the sight of Dimitri. It was obvious that he thought she had gone upstairs and had no idea she was still around.

She froze. Noted the way his voice softened. The pleasure on his face. The way he was murmuring in such velvety tones.

He lounged against a bookcase, utterly relaxed and content and then turned so that his back was to the door. But she heard the word he uttered.

'Athena.'

For a moment she stopped breathing. It was unmistakable amid the flow of liquid Greek. And murmured with a breathtaking tenderness that knifed straight through her.

'Avrio,' he said. Tomorrow. She knew that much Greek.

She walked in, unheard on the thick carpet, intending to ask what was going on. That was when she saw the birthday card. Blinking in disbelief, she stared blankly at the cheerful elephant holding three balloons. There was a cake in front of the animal, with three candles on it, and a badge marked with the number three. It could be for any child he knew, she reasoned, trying to stop her heart from beating so hard and fast it physically hurt.

Or, she thought in growing dismay, it might be a card for Athena's child. *Dimitri's* child. After all, it had been three years ago that she'd seen him lovingly helping Athena into his car.

The woman's forehead had been slicked with sweat. They had paused while her contractions made her gasp and Dimitri had kissed Athena's beautiful face and held her firmly in his strong arms, murmuring something soothing and encouraging.

Everything he'd done, every look he'd given Athena, had shown the love he felt for his pregnant mistress. Wouldn't any man be the same? she had thought at the time. His child was about to be born. A time of joy and masculine pride. A time of tenderness.

Olivia winced. She had been frozen with horror, unable to move or speak. After all, she had been married for six months. That meant he'd known his mistress was pregnant when he'd walked down the aisle between those wreaths of white flowers linked by satin ribbon. When he had been exhorted to love her as if she were his own body. Lies. All lies. All deceit.

She had stared at Dimitri and Athena, a thousand thoughts racing through the turmoil of her mind. During their wedding, all the time they had circled the altar whilst being pelted with rose petals, sugared almonds and rice, had he thought of Athena and his child growing in her womb?

Tortured by this, Olivia had half fallen out of the car after Dimitri had driven away with his pregnant mistress. She had been violently sick. The man she had idolised and respected and loved so deeply had proved to be worthless and shallow. She had battered her fists on the car until the pain was too much to bear any more. But she hadn't cried. Her anger had been too intense for tears.

She feared that Athena might be still in the picture. If so, he had lied to her yet again.

She took a shuddering breath, her sad eyes lingering on Dimitri's gently angled head. Obviously he must feel some kind of love for the mother of his child. But she wondered if this might be the future wife he'd spoken about, the woman he must persuade Marina to accept one day.

Her world seemed to tilt and then steady again. She winced, remembering that she had been close to declaring her own love—and unwittingly facing the humiliation of Dimitri's rejection.

Without a word she crept out, emotion filling her throat like a hard pebble. Tears began to sting her eyes and she found herself stumbling through the hall, half tripping over her own feet.

'Olivia!'

Silently she groaned at Marina's peremptory tone. Dimitri's mother was the next-to-last person she wanted to see at this moment. Incapable of speaking, she flapped a hand of dismissal in her mother-in-law's direction and continued on her way.

'Are you drunk? What is the matter with you?' Marina persisted.

'Dimitri! Who else?' she flung wretchedly, and headed blindly for the stairs.

'Wait.' Marina caught her arm and spun her around.

'No! Leave me alone!' Desperate for somewhere quiet to nurse her wounds, she tried to wrench away, but her mother-in-law was surprisingly strong and determined.

'I want to know what he's done,' Marina said sharply. 'I insist.'

'So you can enjoy my misery?' Olivia shot.

'No. Because I want him to be as happy as I am.'

Olivia slumped in capitulation. Why not tell her? What did it matter any more?

'Not here,' she jerked out, feeling venomous. She glared at the study door. 'The way I'm feeling, if he comes out of there I might damage his face permanently.'

Marina registered shock. 'Come into the salon,' she ordered hastily. 'I think I should know what is going on.'

Imprisoned by the firm fingers that held her wrist in a vice-like grip, Olivia trailed after the thin, upright figure into the sunny room. She knew that she had to be careful what she said. If Marina knew the marriage was really over now, then that would leave Eleni free to pester him. It would be ages before the divorce came through and she'd be stuck in Greece, with her life on hold.

And yet... Olivia paled. They couldn't continue with their ridiculous pretence. Not now. It would be unbearable, living here day after day, exchanging kisses and loving looks with him. Even worse to watch him drive away, wondering if he was heading for Athena's arms. She just couldn't trust him.

Hell, she thought grimly, he wouldn't know love if

it were burnt with a hot poker in capital letters on his
steel-hard heart.

'I'm waiting.'

Olivia heaved in a hard, hurting lungful of air.
Determined to keep the angry tears at bay, she lifted
her chin.

'I—I had thought that Dimitri and I might be able
to forget the past and start again—'

'So he said at breakfast. Don't you love him after
all?'

'No,' she said flatly. 'I don't.'

Marina's eyes widened. 'So I was right all along!'

'Not exactly. I really thought he'd changed. But I'm
not sure any more. Sometimes I think he might have
the morals of an alley cat.'

'It sounds as if you hate him,' Marina said.

'I do!' she hurled emphatically.

'So tell me, if you hate him, why are you upset?'
her mother-in-law demanded. 'Is it because you've lost
the chance to live a life of luxury again?'

'No!' Olivia yelled. 'Because I love him to distrac-
tion!'

'I'm confused. The note you left when you disappeared said the opposite,' Marina pointed out.

Olivia frowned. 'No, it didn't. I said there wasn't
any point in staying when *he* didn't love me! Heavens
above, you saw how devastated I was when I saw him
with his mistress! I've always loved him, more fool
me. I know what you thought. That I went after him
because he was rich. Well, I didn't know that he was
wealthy to begin with. We went to small, intimate restaurants. His apartment was functional rather than luxurious. He drove an expensive car—but then a lot of
men go into debt to get the car of their dreams. And

by the time I knew he actually headed the vast Angelaki empire I was madly in love and I didn't care what or who he was, so long as we could be together.

'I'm stupid enough to have fallen for him, like all the other women who worship him and leap into his bed whenever he crooks his finger! Every time I'm with him I think that I'm the only woman in the world for him and it's the most wonderful feeling I've ever known. He has me dangling on a string and dancing to his tune like some wretched puppet. But I've got feelings, Marina! I love him and I hate him because he can hurt me so deeply that I can barely bring myself to continue living!' She put a hand to her aching forehead. 'I have to go,' she said weakly. 'I can't allow myself to stay near him. He's destroying me, inch by inch. I have to be shot of him. And I want you to help me to find somewhere to live in Greece while I'm waiting for the divorce. I'm sure you'll be willing,' she added with bitterness.

Her mother-in-law seemed stunned by Olivia's outburst. 'I—I had no idea you felt like that,' she said eventually. There was a long silence.

'You believe me?' Olivia mumbled.

'Yes,' Marina said softly. 'I recognise what you are saying. I felt the same about my Theo.' She smiled when Olivia blinked in surprise. 'Yes. The Angelaki men have a habit of rejecting the love of their wives. You left my son because you'd been hurt by his affair with that woman we saw—'

'I think he's still seeing her.' Olivia tried unsuccessfully to hide her pain. 'Perhaps because of their child. Perhaps because… ' She couldn't bring herself to say any more of her fears.

Marina frowned hard. 'My dear, I'm going to give you some advice that might surprise you.'

'I want practical help, not advice,' Olivia muttered.

To her surprise, her mother-in-law's eyes softened. 'You'll get it. But...first, something that will interest you... It may astonish you to know how awful Dimitri has been since you left. Bad-tempered, difficult to please, with little time for friends or family.'

'Why are you telling me this?' she asked.

'Because Nikos has been talking to me about you. He thinks well of you and I trust his judgement. So I'm telling you that Dimitri was deeply affected by your disappearance.'

What did she care? She shrugged. 'I imagine his pride was hurt.'

'Or maybe he was devastated when you left and wanted you back.' Marina sighed. 'Who knows? All I can say is that he was not happy and his mistress was obviously not giving him what he wanted. However, he has been happy since you returned. I will tell you this. If you truly love him then you must accept him as he is.'

'An unfaithful cheat?' Olivia spluttered.

'You wouldn't be the first to turn a blind eye to adultery,' Marina said, an unhappy light in her dark eyes. She hesitated. 'Olivia, I know my Theo had a mistress somewhere. But I saw no reason to leave him just because he'd found a younger woman sexier than me.'

Olivia stared in amazement. 'You didn't mind?'

'Of course I did. But I wanted him,' she said simply.

It seemed an awful compromise. And she wondered if that was why Marina seemed so bitter about life. 'Were you happy at all?' she asked gently, astonished that her mother-in-law had told her such an intimate confidence.

There was a fleeting flash of anguish tightening the gaunt face. 'No,' she admitted. 'And I confess I probably made him miserable with my sharp tongue and drove him even further from me. But I couldn't help it, I loved and needed him so much. Maybe I even drove him to another woman's arms in the first place. I was intensely possessive.'

Olivia could feel Marina's sorrow because she knew the same pain of rejection and humiliation. On an impulse, she put her arms around her mother-in-law in an understanding hug.

'I couldn't do what you did. You're much stronger than me,' she confided.

'Or more pig-headed,' Marina said with a rueful sigh. She pushed away slightly and looked at Olivia with sympathy as she tucked an escaped strand of hair behind Olivia's ear in an almost gentle, motherly gesture. 'But I couldn't bear being cast aside so I pretended not to know the truth. It seems that Dimitri is like his father. Let him have his freedom. You must decide on your course of action. Either divorce him— or stay married and ignore his absences.'

Olivia gazed at Marina helplessly. 'I can't live without him,' she admitted. 'Yet I can't live *with* him if he's having affairs. Or even one affair. How could I lie in bed wondering if he was coming home, wondering who he was with? It would crucify me. And yet I don't really feel I'm alive without him. Oh, Marina!' she whispered, as the finality of the situation began to hit home. 'I have to go. Help me, I beg you—'

'There you are!' The two women jumped at the sound of Dimitri's strong voice. He stared in amazement at their friendly embrace. 'What on earth is going on?'

Olivia's mouth tightened into a thin, hard line. 'Character assassination on my part.'

He looked puzzled by her hostility. And so sublimely innocent that her knees automatically weakened. He was utterly desirable to her as he pushed a hand through his silky hair and it tumbled boyishly onto his broad forehead.

'But...I thought you... We were going out somewhere today—'

'Oh, is that still on?' she asked coolly. 'I imagined you had better things to do or other people to see.'

There was a tightening of his face. His lashes dipped and lifted again and he shot his mother a sharp glance. To Olivia, he looked taken aback—and highly embarrassed. Proof, if she needed it, of his guilt.

'The phone call! Of course. I'm sorry I had to leave you.' He smiled with agonisingly tender affection and she melted, as she always did, her heart pounding with love, her head, however, bursting with ungovernable anger. 'But I'm here now, and we have the day ahead of us. You choose where we're going—'

'*We* are going nowhere. I am leaving this house and getting out of your life for good,' she said, ice dripping from every word.

He was instantly alert. 'Leaving? I don't think so,' he sliced at her.

Tactfully, Marina muttered something and slipped from the room past the granite-faced Dimitri.

'Watch!' Olivia spat out.

He folded his arms across his chest, his entire body taut with menace. 'Care to tell me the reason for your change of mind?'

'With pleasure! I'm sick and tired,' she ground out, 'of being used by you!'

'You might be tired but that, I imagine, is because you were unusually enthusiastic last night,' he growled, looking offended that she'd apparently forgotten the eager part she had played.

'I like sex!' she hurled. Liked? Adored it passionately—with him—until she had come to her senses after that phone call and realised that she was probably nothing but a toy for him to play with!

Dimitri's eyes narrowed. She had reduced a memorable day and night to basic lust. His heart pounded as he realised with mounting dismay that for him it had been a deeper experience. Fool that he was. He knew she had never loved him. She'd made that perfectly clear.

His fists clenched. Every instinct was now driving him to punish her. To exact some kind of revenge. He would break her. He had to. No woman was going to treat him with such contempt.

'You don't need to tell me you like sex. I'd noticed for myself,' he drawled.

She flushed. 'I respond to you because you're good at it. I hear that comes of continual practice. But what we did last night doesn't mean I like you, or that I accept your peculiar morality—'

'Just a minute. What has my mother said?' Putting two and two together, he moved forward, till he was just a foot away, studying her with shrewd eyes. Olivia had radically changed her mind about their arrangement. There could be only one explanation. 'I thought she was happy for me that you were staying. But…has she offered you money to go?'

Olivia gasped and cracked her hand across his face.

He caught it a second too late, and for a moment she was terrified by the black glitter in his eyes. Then he did something extraordinary. He pulled her against him, tipped her head back roughly and kissed her hard.

She fought him—and herself. Felt her body sliding against his. The fierce beat of his heart. He cupped one breast and bent her backwards, dominating her, firing her with his skilful, hateful caresses till she sank into them, her defiance blown away by her own body's betrayal.

'You want me!' he gritted. 'That's obvious. OK. We'll deal. Shall I offer you even more money to stay?'

Olivia drew her head back, hot blue eyes blazing into his. 'I can't be bought or bribed!' she grated. 'I don't want your mother's money or yours—'

'You took the maintenance I sent you,' he said in a cynical drawl.

Her eyes widened in utter bewilderment. 'What maintenance?'

'Paid into the English bank where we had a joint account, remember? Or was that small change for you?' he scathed.

'You don't know which bank I use! I go to a different one in—' She firmed her mouth, remembering not to tell him where she'd been for the past three years. 'If you've put money in our old bank,' she said grimly, 'then it's still there untouched, with the rest of the cash we'd put by. There are probably statements heaped up on the mat of your London apartment. Haven't you been there?'

'No. Avoided it like the plague,' he muttered. His eyes narrowed. 'Are you telling me you haven't taken a penny?'

She applauded. 'Well done.'

He scowled at her sarcasm but he looked uncomfortable. 'I thought—'

'I know what you thought,' she snapped. 'That I worship money.'

'Don't you?'

'No more than the next woman. Of course I like new clothes and eating in restaurants and trips to New York. Of course it was wonderful to have financial security. But that came at a price—'

'Me.'

'You,' she agreed, deciding not to elaborate any more.

His mouth tightened. 'How did you manage when you left?'

She glared. 'I told you. On my own earnings. I don't need a man to provide for me. Does that tell you something about my money-grabbing tactics? Does that suggest I might *not* have taken a bribe from your mother?'

Clearly surprised, he touched his face where the marks of her fingers still lingered. 'I deserved this, it seems,' he said stiffly.

'And more!' she muttered.

His eyes flashed but he nodded. 'I apologise. However, it doesn't explain why you are so determined to leave. Only last night you seemed perfectly reconciled to amusing yourself with me for an indefinite period.'

'And now I want to go home,' she muttered, not daring to tell him that his cavalier attitude to women distressed her. He might think she cared—and that was the last thing she wanted him to know.

'This is an attempt to wring more alimony out of me, isn't it? Yes,' he said when she opened her mouth to protest, 'I know you haven't touched the maintenance, but that's because you didn't know it was there. The fact remains that you admit you like financial security. Your lawyer has already accepted a substantial sum on your behalf which you want to increase—'

'I don't want it!' she snapped.

His eyebrow arced up in surprise. 'Really? Then ring him. I am calling your bluff, Olivia.'

'I don't know what time it is—'

'Excuses, excuses.'

'All right!' Eyes glittering, she picked up the phone on his desk and made the call, instructing the astonished Paul that she didn't want one penny from Dimitri.

'He's forced you to do this!' Paul protested. 'Olivia, if he's seduced you with the sole purpose of—'

'Maybe he has, maybe he hasn't,' she snapped. 'I don't care any more. I just want to wash my hands of everything connected with him as soon as I possibly can. I refuse to be accused of whoring. As far as I'm concerned, whatever has the Angelaki stamp on it is contaminated and poisonous.' Shaking, she put the receiver down. 'Satisfied?' she flung at Dimitri. 'You can't accuse me of marrying you for your money now. Or divorcing you for it.'

'Why the devil did you marry me, then?' he flung angrily.

'If you don't know, I sure as hell am not going to tell you!' she yelled.

He went very still. His eyes searched hers. 'Love?'

It was the way he said the word that made her tremble, imbuing it with such tenderness that she felt her heart would break.

'Love,' she agreed, her face mournful. 'It's terrible when it dies.'

So that was it. She had loved him once—maybe in

the early days of their relationship. But when they were married she'd been restless. After she'd run away, the passage of time must have killed whatever feelings she'd once had for him. At least now he knew the truth and could act accordingly. She would regret ever giving him the impression that their love had been reignited.

His teeth clenched. She looked suddenly vulnerable, her lashes thick crescents on her cheeks. Her mouth seemed carved in sorrow and he had the urge to kiss it into smiles. Instead, he scowled and sought to bind her to him. Because he wasn't finished with her yet.

'We're getting nowhere. The plain fact is that you can't leave,' he said in cutting tones, 'because you would be breaking your promise.'

She stared at him in loathing. 'I didn't promise that I'd live here!'

'No,' he said, his mouth savage. 'But you agreed that you'd pretend we were in love until Eleni gave up her quest to be the next Mrs Angelaki. And lovers don't live in separate places, not if they're married and rebuilding their relationship.'

She swallowed the ache in her throat. Tried to ignore the nausea swirling around in her stomach. He looked utterly ruthless and determined. The set of his body and the hardness of his eyes intimidated her. He actually wanted her to stay around and flatter his ego in bed and out of it, while she slowly died inside!

'You can't and you won't hold me to that!' she cried, distraught.

'Believe me, I can and I will,' he growled, his brows a dark line above coal-black eyes. 'It was a promise. And one I'll make you keep.'

'I can't bear to be near you!' she cried raggedly.

His eyes flashed a warning, and then his hands descended on her shoulders as if intent on crushing her slender bones.

'Do it,' he gritted. 'You want this farce of a marriage annulled in record time. It's the only way.'

'I can't keep the pretence going! I feel sick at the thought of being touched by you—'

'Then,' he said, frighteningly tight and angry, 'I have to congratulate you on your performance to date. You almost convinced me that you enjoyed every second.'

'Let me go,' she said feebly.

'No. You won't wriggle out of this.'

She gave a helpless groan. 'Please, Dimitri!'

'Nothing would give me more pleasure than to see the back of you,' he snapped. 'But you have a job to do. I'll make it easier for you, though. You will continue to live here. We will leave for trips together and return together. This place is a hotbed of gossip and Eleni will soon discover that we are rarely separated—'

'I'm not spending all day with you—'

'You'll do whatever I say,' he growled. 'At night—'

'I won't sleep with you!'

'I can't remember us sleeping much before,' he said drily. 'But I agree. You will sleep in my room for appearances' sake, but I will go elsewhere—'

'Where?' she demanded, thinking of Athena.

'Anywhere. Does it matter?' he said impatiently. 'Agree to this and I'll get my lawyers working around the clock. You'll soon be free of me. And I will be free of you,' he finished under his breath.

If only she hadn't given her word. He had trapped her in an impossible situation. She lifted a haunted face.

'I have no choice,' she muttered. And ran from the room before she burst into tears.

CHAPTER NINE

THE boat sped once again across the aquamarine sea, leaving behind the small community where her happiness had been found and lost for the second time. The white houses faded against the background of olive trees covering the hills and soon the harbour and the little boats there were no longer visible.

The contrast between how she felt on this day and how she had felt the previous day was too painful to contemplate.

She knew that Eleni had watched them leave the house from the drawing-room window. And Olivia had felt a pang of sympathy for her, knowing what that misery was like and how horribly it could possess and destroy. She didn't like what she was doing—and wished it were all over.

They headed for a sickle-shaped beach backed by tamarisk trees where they had spent many glorious hours in the past. She tried hard not to think of those days. What was the point? They'd been a fantasy strictly of her own making, after all.

Dimitri killed the engine and let the boat drift on the gentle swell towards the shore. Like her, he wore beige shorts, though his T-shirt was blue not white, and more close-fitting, hugging the contours of his broad chest.

He might have been a fisherman but for his imperious manner that marked him out as a man used to being obeyed. With a shiver of apprehension she watched him leap into the crystal water. The muscles

of his arms stood out as he hauled the boat further up
the beach and she jerked her head away to stare at the
distant islands out to sea because she didn't want to
moon over him any more. Those days were over.

'Take my hand.'

So many times they had done this. She had ended
up in those strong, supposedly loving arms and they
had kissed and murmured their adoration while the water swirled around their legs.

'No.'

Determined to be independent of him, she stood up,
preparing to jump into the shallow water.

'Olivia,' he snapped, 'she can see us from the
house.' He jerked his head at the promontory. Of
course she knew that. She could easily make out the
mansion rising from the trees. 'Just do it.'

She did. With bad grace. And she didn't know how
it happened, but one minute she was upright, the next
she had fallen into two feet of water. On top of Dimitri.
They surfaced, spluttering. His arms held her securely.
Too securely.

For a moment she responded, her mouth seeking his
in a terrible knee-jerk reaction. How wrong could her
instincts be?

'Very good,' he rasped, fastening his mouth greedily
on hers.

She could feel the anger in him and fought to be
free, gasping when the water swirled over their partly
submerged bodies.

'That'll do.'

Abruptly he let her go. Clamping his hands on her
waist, he hauled her up. Water streamed down his con-
torted face. His eyes were small black chips of glass,
his mouth a tight, grim line.

She had never seen him so close to losing control. He bit out a single word with frightening venom. *'Bitch.'*

Blindly she staggered to the shore and concentrated on twisting her hair to wring out the water. She was trembling, afraid of what he would do. And suddenly she knew she couldn't stay here all day, in full sight of the house. He'd be demanding that they gave a convincing performance of two lovers enjoying themselves and she shuddered to think how far he expected her to go.

'I refuse to sit on a beach all day while you pretend to make advances and Eleni watches, poor girl,' she said stubbornly. 'I'm not an exhibit. And I won't have you grope me more than you have to! Take me somewhere else.'

With a mutter of irritation, he swept his palms over his wet face and shot, 'Where, then?'

'I don't know. Anywhere would be hell,' she snapped.

'Helpful,' he clipped.

Her temper flared. 'If we *have* to go anywhere together, I'd prefer a drive into the hills. I can sit on one side of a mountain and you can sit on the other, out of my sight,' she said coldly.

'You're right,' he growled to her surprise. 'I'd prefer not to touch you. Get into the boat. We'll return to the house and change our clothes—and our destination.'

Mutely she obeyed. In a horrible, deadly silence, they returned to the harbour. Clearly in a filthy mood, Dimitri helped her to the quayside.

'Face me.'

'No.'

Ruthlessly he grabbed her arms and stared into her

mutinous eyes. 'A few minutes of simpering, that's all we need,' he bit. 'My arm around you while we walk to the house. Your head leaning on my shoulder. And if you imagine I'm enjoying this, then think again. I have finally discovered what you are, Olivia. A cold-hearted little tramp who seeks only to satisfy her own selfish needs.'

'And you,' she slashed, 'are a swaggering bully, with no concept of love or decency, who must hate women because all you do is betray them and hurt them!'

His arm wrapped around her waist. Stiffly they moved up the little road. Olivia knew she couldn't keep this up. Being with him like this was a living night-mare.

To her relief, there was no sign of Eleni when they reached the house. When Dimitri enquired, he was told that she had gone out with a young man in a sports car. Perhaps their ruse was working. She hoped so.

Walking indoors, she changed into a blue cotton sun-dress and met Dimitri by the garage block.

'I suppose this stupid trip is necessary?' she asked haughtily.

'I wouldn't be doing it otherwise. I'd rather be sitting behind my desk dealing with a mountain of mail,' he snapped. 'But I'm prepared to do this to get you out of my hair. Get in.'

He looked cool in stone cotton jeans and T-shirt, but when their fingers brushed as he opened the car door for her she discovered that his skin was burning hot. She snatched her hand away and cradled it on her lap as if it had been scorched.

The moment Dimitri flung himself into the driver's seat she felt crowded. A hurried, slanting glance at his granite face told her that the hostility between them had reached epic proportions.

Silent and rigid with tension, she cringed back in the seat and clipped on the safety belt. He drove with grim concentration into the mountains. Miserably she stared out of the window, hardly noticing the scenery. Ruined classical temples flashed by. Tiny domed churches, secret villages designed to be hidden from marauders and the Ottoman tax collectors. The road zigzagged up a steep hill terraced with vineyards and they only came to a stop when a flock of goats blocked their way.

'Health to your hands,' Dimitri said courteously to the men amiably moving the goats along, and smiles and greetings returned his traditional acknowledgement.

It was sickening the way everybody adored and admired him, she thought bitterly. He was a fraud. A man without a heart.

The car crawled along at a snail's pace till Olivia felt like screaming. Her head ached from the tension and misery she was keeping under tight control. This hideous situation was making her ill and she resented that.

'Where are we going?' she muttered through her teeth.

'I've no idea.'

She drew in a sharp breath. 'Find somewhere quickly where we can stop. I'm not spending the whole day cooped up in this car with you.'

'I'm killing time. If you have any ideas, then share them,' he said sarcastically.

'Any hill will do, providing you're on the other side of it!' she muttered.

He stabbed a hard finger at the radio. The soft strains

of a sad love song murmured through the icy silence. Olivia closed her eyes, squeezing them tightly to stop the tears from escaping. Unable to bear the tug on her emotions any longer, she punched the 'off' button and slumped back miserably in the seat.

He shot her a quick glance and wished he hadn't. Her lashes were wet with tears and there was a telltale shiny trail shimmering down her cheek to the corner of her mouth. Why her distress should upset him, he didn't know. But it did. He wanted to scoop her up into his arms and soothe her, to say that everything would be all right—when he knew full well that in a few days they'd be parting for ever.

And what of his revenge? He had meant to make her dependent on him. To hunger for him and beg to be loved in return. Then he had intended to reject her so that she knew what it was like to feel passionately for someone and be callously dismissed, as she had dismissed him. But now he couldn't do that. His feelings were too raw, his own emotions too disturbed. She was slowly destroying him. All his instincts were telling him to call a halt to the charade they'd agreed to play. He couldn't stand this disruption of his mind and body any longer.

'Olivia,' he began huskily.

A movement told him that she had averted her head. Quickly estimating where they were, he pulled off at the next turning and drove down a bumpy track. They had to work out a strategy for ending this as soon—and as painlessly—as they could.

Nikos was already lining up eligible young men for Eleni—and apparently she had dates every night that week. He was sure that soon she would no longer be a problem.

That meant he could risk putting Olivia on the plane home that evening. As that thought permeated his consciousness, his eyes widened at the sharp contraction in his chest. Astonishingly, his head seemed to explode with pain. And he screeched to a stop in a flurry of dust and burning rubber.

'What?' yelled Olivia, clutching her chest. 'What on earth are you doing? You nearly broke my ribs!'

Slowly he turned, dazed, stunned by his realisation. In her anger she looked unbelievably beautiful, her huge blue eyes fixed on him in searing fury. There were small freckles on her gold-tinged nose, winging across her cheekbones in such a heartbreakingly appealing way that he felt his hand move out to touch them before he knew what he was doing.

'Keep your hands off me!' she stormed, slapping it away. 'And explain why you're practising emergency stops!'

Such a soft mouth. Designed for kissing. The heat in his loins intensified and he had to look away. He needed to think. To talk to her. To put an outrageous suggestion to her.

The risk to his pride was incalculable, but if he didn't he'd never forgive himself.

'I'm sorry. I had an idea,' he croaked, his mouth dry with nerves.

'Let's hope it involves imminent separation.'

Muttering something rude under her breath, she folded her arms and waited for him to drive on.

It took a moment before he could clear his brain and find the gearstick. When he did, his gaze lingered on the long, tanned length of her leg and he knew he'd do anything to keep her.

Olivia felt the heat of his eyes and tugged her skirt

down over her thigh. 'Don't even think it,' she snapped.

Without a word, he put the car into gear and drove on carefully down the rutted track, at the end of which he parked.

'I think we should talk,' he said quietly.

'Is that so? First, I don't trust you,' she muttered. 'Second, it's a bit late for that. Third, I have nothing to say.'

'I have, though. I think I will surprise you.'

A quick glance at his face told her what she'd feared on hearing his low, seductive tones.

'You sit here and surprise yourself, then,' she said, flinging open the door. 'I'm going for a walk. Alone.'

The way her body moved as she strode away just made his breath choke in his throat. She held herself proudly, the tilt of her beautiful head a little too high on that slender neck. The stiff swing of her arms and the jerky movements of her legs were touchingly child-like in their anger. That, more than anything else, made his heart do a small skip.

There was no woman like Olivia. Dazed, he watched the resolute figure of his wife, with her blonde hair flying in the breeze, and prepared to use every weapon at his disposal to persuade her to stay.

When she reached the top of a small rise Olivia found herself looking down on a small circular theatre, rather like the one at Epidauros but with only ten rows of marble seats. It had been poorly preserved and had become overgrown with scrub and wild flowers, though the central court—where the actors had stood perhaps two thousand years earlier—was still intact.

Determined to while away the time until she could return to the privacy of her own room at the mansion, she began to walk around the upper rim, blanking her mind to everything.

The tread of her feet disturbed brightly coloured lizards, their quick, darting movements making it look as if they were jewels flashing in the bright sun. As she brushed the low bushes of thyme and velvety sage their leaves released powerful oils, scenting the air heavily.

Her heart jerked. She would miss so much. There would be perhaps one or two days left here and then she would be going home. Away from Dimitri...

The pain in her bruised heart stole her breath, and she sat down on the cold marble seat. Everything had been so perfect. Dimitri, the love she'd thought they'd shared, this beautiful, fierce blue sky, the warmth of the sun on her aching body, the fabulous views and fascinating history.

'I want you to listen to me, Olivia.'

She blinked and looked down to the source of the voice. Dimitri stood in the circular court below, as he had in Epidauros that fatal day when he'd said he loved her—shortly before she had discovered him with Athena. The acoustics were perfect. Although he spoke quietly, she could hear every word.

Coldly she stared down at his dark head. He had nothing to say that would touch her. Not now.

'It doesn't matter that you don't love me,' he said, his face lifted up to where she stood. She tensed. He looked as if he was pleading with her. 'The fact is...' He sighed, with a helpless spread of his hands. 'I don't think I can bear it if you go...'

Liar! Rage and pain seared through her. Turning her head away, she tightened her jaw. Now what? Did he need half an hour of sex? She would have left him there, spouting his lies, but she felt suddenly bone-tired. Let him ramble on. It wouldn't make any difference.

'...and when it dawned on me that you'd be almost certain to leave in a day or two, I...'

Oh, clever, she thought, jerking her head back to see what fake attitude he was adopting now. Contemptuously she noted the dipped head, the clearing of his throat. What an actor he would have made. If she didn't know any better, she would have been convinced of his misery.

Especially when he raised his head. Even from where she sat it was possible to see that his eyes were shining a little too brightly. Her tender heart contracted, and then she came to her senses and anger once again filled every cell in her body. Hard-eyed, she let him continue, to see how far he'd go to get what he wanted.

'It's true, Olivia. I can't live without you!' he blurted out throatily. 'Do what you like here. Live where you like, so long as it's not too far away. But let me see you sometimes. Let me prove to you that...' His chest rose high and fell again, and she heard the long hiss of his breath as it emptied his lungs. 'Olivia,' he cried in ringing tones, 'I love you more deeply than I ever imagined. I always have, always will. Let me love you. Take care of you.' He knelt on the dusty stone floor, and she stared at him, mesmerised. 'I do love you, Olivia. With every inch of my body, every breath I take, every thought in my head. I want you to be the mother of my children—'

She jumped to her feet, unable to stand any more. And she walked back to the car. Too late, she thought unhappily. He was making his pitch at the wrong time, because it just hurt her to hear him protesting his love, to be offered the chance to bear his children.

Stumbling, she tripped and fell onto the stony track with a cry of pain as her head hit a small rock. For a moment she lay there, all the stuffing knocked out of her by Dimitri's cruel pretence. And suddenly he was with her, gently turning her over, gathering her into his arms.

'Leave me!' she moaned, and thudded her fists weakly into his chest.

'You're hurt,' he said in a choking whisper.

His finger lightly explored her forehead and she winced, her eyes narrowing at his devastated expression. Why would he look so miserable? It didn't make sense. Unless he was upset at being turned down.

'Anything else damaged?' he enquired, still croaky.

Her heart. It had been smashed beyond all repair, she wanted to tell him. But he was gently rubbing at her elbows and the heels of her hands, which were white with road dust, and she had to bite her lip to stop herself from releasing a small sob of self-pity.

Because the care and concern in his expression just made her ache.

'I want to go back,' she said in a tone as dead as her eyes. 'I don't want to do this any more. I've reached my limit.'

'Of course.' He swallowed and looked at her as if his world had come to an end. 'I love you, Olivia,' he jerked hoarsely.

She turned her head away and stared coldly into the mid-distance. After a moment his hands slid away and he helped her to her feet.

'There's a first-aid kit in the car,' he muttered.

Snatching her arm away from his supporting hand, she grimly stomped back along the track. Mentally she left the beauties of Greece, and one Greek in particular, far behind.

When he came up to where she sat on the ground, with the first-aid kit on her lap, she pointedly ignored him and continued to dab at her forehead with the calendula cream. The silence seemed to crush her like a heavy weight. Briefly she looked up at him, to see why he was standing there, staring at her, and she stopped breathing.

His face was dead. The vitality and vibrancy had gone. His skin had a greyish tint and his eyes were no longer a gleaming black but a cold, muddy brown. The liveliness of his mobile mouth had become a pained, downturned line. And the change in him made her want to cry.

'You drive,' he growled.

She blinked as he spun on his heel and sat in the passenger seat. Slowly she got to her feet, stunned by the extraordinary way that Dimitri's vigour had ebbed from his body. And for the life of her she couldn't understand why—unless it was because he feared that marriage to Eleni was inevitable now.

It wasn't until they drove up to the mansion that Dimitri spoke again. 'I'll arrange a flight for you to England this evening,' he said in strangled tones. 'My jet is in Paris. It'll have to be a commercial airline.'

'Fine.' Numb with misery, she crawled out of the car. To her surprise, he immediately moved behind the wheel. 'Where are you going?' she blurted out in astonishment, alarmed that he would be driving in his odd state of mind.

'I don't think it's any of your business,' he said wearily, and stamped his foot viciously on the accelerator.

She stared after him in consternation. And in a flash

of inspiration she knew where he could be heading. To Athena, the ever-loving mother of his child, who'd stood by him all these years.

Olivia's eyes took on the colour of slate. She fished out the car keys he'd given her and grimly marched to the garage block.

All the time he'd been slinging her that line about loving her—and looking as if he believed every wretched word—he had fully intended to keep Athena on, as a back-up.

Well, she thought, her fingers gripping the wheel as if it were her lifeline, she would confront him at Athena's house and then he'd be forced to admit that everything he'd said was a lie.

CHAPTER TEN

ATHENA stroked his forehead, but her gentle fingers did nothing to smooth the deep furrows there. The pain was too deep. Unreachable.

She had gasped when she'd opened the door to her cottage. Stumbling in, almost drunk from the turmoil raging around in his mind, he'd caught a glimpse of himself in a mirror and had realised why she was so shocked.

He hardly recognised himself in the zombie who stared back with graveyard eyes. Love and Olivia had done this to him.

Now he sat listlessly at Athena's feet in the garden overlooking Selonda Bay, two glasses of wine poured and forgotten, while little Theo played happily with his toy cars.

Warm and loving as always, Athena asked no questions but waited for him to speak. He didn't know where to begin. His future seemed utterly bleak and uninviting. He would have done anything for Olivia. Given her whatever she wanted. And she'd turned him down.

Bone-weary from hurling his emotions into a void, only to have them slung back at him, he leaned his head back against Athena's knees and closed his eyes. But he still saw Olivia. If it was anything like the last time she left him he'd see her there for a long while.

He groaned. Lightly Athena's fingers caressed his face. And then they stilled abruptly.

Looking up, Dimitri was astonished to see Olivia. He blinked, thinking he must be hallucinating, because she didn't know where Athena lived or where he might have gone, but she was definitely there, by the low gate that led into the garden. She flung it open angrily and strode towards him, her face set, hair streaming behind her in golden waves.

'What a pretty scene!' she scorned. 'And you claim you love me?'

'Yes,' was all he could manage—and that was hardly coherent.

'You're living in a make-believe world, Dimitri!' she flashed. 'Get real. While you're with one woman you love her. You honestly seem to believe that. Then five minutes later you're with some other lover—and you offer undying love to *her!* It's not normal,' she snapped. 'Either you know full well what you're doing, in which case you're the lowest form of life that exists, or you are deluded, in which case you need a psychiatrist—'

'I don't have any confusion,' he husked. 'I love you. It's that simple.'

Olivia seemed shocked. She looked at Athena and then back at him again. 'You can say that in front of her? I can't understand how Greek women accept infidelity so easily,' she jerked.

'They don't,' Athena said quietly. 'What are you trying to say, Olivia?'

At the gentleness in the other woman's voice, Olivia's eyes filled with tears.

'I loved him!' she sobbed. 'He was everything to me! And when I came back to Greece and saw him again I knew I would always feel that way! Then he lied to me and deceived me and pretended he cared when all the time he was two-timing me! I can't bear it! And I hate being so feeble and crying like this over such a louse!' She rounded on Dimitri. 'You've broken my heart! I hope you'll be miserable as hell and some woman will hurt you as you've hurt me...'

She broke down in a storm of weeping. Athena hurried to her and led her inside the cottage, frantically waving Dimitri back when he made to follow.

'This is my bathroom,' she said gently to Olivia. 'You can freshen up here and then we can talk. Dimitri isn't the kind of man you claim he is—'

'See him for what he is! You've been taken in by him, as I was!'

Olivia wrenched on the tap and glared at Athena in the mirror. The woman was older than she'd seemed from a distance. Perhaps forty-five, with several grey hairs. Probably good in bed, Olivia thought bitterly. She sluiced her face and dried it.

And then she noticed a photograph of Athena with Dimitri. No, not Dimitri...

Olivia whirled, and went to study the snapshot. It showed Athena and Dimitri's *father*, Theo, looking adoringly at each other. She held her breath in shock and looked around. On a shelf was a photo of Theo, smiling into the camera with that besotted look adopted by all lovers.

She strode into the adjoining bedroom and swallowed hard. There were pictures everywhere. Theo on a beach somewhere, laughing. Theo...

Wide-eyed, she spun around to stare at the puzzled Athena. 'Dimitri's father?' she breathed.

Athena smiled fondly and stroked one of the photos. 'My darling Theo,' she said softly.

It was too much for Olivia. She went outside and

faced the tense-looking Dimitri, who was standing by a wrought-iron table, a glass of wine in his hand. When he saw her, he drained the glass and put it down, a wary expression on his face. No wonder he seemed agitated, she thought in contempt.

'Whose child is that?' she demanded.

Dimitri frowned. 'I can't tell you.'

'I will.' Athena spoke up. 'He is Theo's child. But Marina must never know. We don't want to hurt her. I hope you will not tell her our secret—it would be too cruel.'

Shaken, Olivia tried to steady herself. Dimitri's morals were worse than she'd ever imagined.

'I don't believe you two! Is it a Greek tradition to take on your father's mistress?' she demanded angrily.

He blinked. Very slowly, a smile spread across his face, and then he was laughing with Athena, who was doubled up and clutching him as if she had never heard anything so funny in the whole of her life.

Their easy intimacy outraged her, and she had to sit down on a low wall because of the cutting pains in her chest. How dared they laugh at her?

She sat with a forlorn expression on her face, though her fists were clenched as if she might attack him at any moment. Dimitri sobered, hating to see her so hurt, so misled.

'Athena isn't my mistress. I've never been her lover—'

'I saw you!' Olivia whispered, her eyes huge and silvered with distress. 'She was in labour and you were helping her into your car—'

'Oh, hell! So that's it!' He groaned, and a wave of regret churned at his stomach. 'How on earth did you find us?'

'Your mother guided me,' she said, her voice taut and strained.

'My...mother?' He and Athena looked at one another in consternation.

'Yes.' Olivia flung up her head defiantly. 'She'd been telling me you had a mistress ever since the day we met. Finally I became suspicious about your secretive phone calls. She offered to take me to your mistress's house.'

Poor Olivia. What she must have thought... 'And that was the day you left—?'

'Of course it was!' she cried, slamming her fist on the hard stone. She winced, and he reached out to take that wounded little hand in his but she glared at him so fiercely that he thought better of it. Her lower lip trembled and his heart somersaulted with love and tenderness.

'Olivia,' he said gently, 'Why didn't you tell me what you'd seen? I could have explained—'

'I wouldn't have believed you!' she hurled tightly. 'You were loving and k-kind to Athena, and it was obvious that she must be the mother of your child... Oh.' She looked confused. 'He's Theo's child. I don't understand.'

'I can assure you that he is Theo's child. And I have never loved or made love to any other man but Theo in the whole of my life. Why don't you two sort this out somewhere private?' Athena suggested, as little Theo ran to her and clung to her knees, his huge Dimitri-eyes round and anxious.

Olivia's hand flew to her mouth. 'I'm sorry! I wouldn't have upset your little boy for the world—'

Jumping to her feet in agitation, Olivia was dazed by Athena's gentle smile.

'It's all right. I'll explain to him,' Athena said. 'Just go. And tell her everything, Dimitri. I mean *everything*,' she added, kissing his cheek and lifting Theo up for a cuddle. Dimitri buried his face in the toddler's little neck and then set about tickling him, till his half-brother giggled, his little face sunny once more.

'Olivia,' he said quietly when he'd set Theo down. 'We have a lot of explaining to do, the two of us. I want to clear the air. Will you trust me and give me an hour of your time?'

Hardly breathing, he waited for her nod, and when it came he felt as if he'd been reprieved from a prison sentence.

His heart pounding, he drove her to the ruined temple by the sea, dedicated to Aphrodite, and they sat on the base of a fallen column, amidst a drift of wild sea lilies, the air heavy with pine scent and herbs.

'I'll begin with Athena. She was from my father's village,' Dimitri said when Olivia looked at him questioningly. 'They'd known one another as children. He always remained a simple, uncomplicated man at heart, loving the land, happy with his old village friends.'

'He was wrong to love her,' Olivia reproved. 'He was married.'

Dimitri sighed. 'Only because he felt he had to marry Mother.'

'What do you mean?' she asked, her curiosity aroused.

'Initially he'd been going out with Marina, and she adored him. But she was a little too possessive, and as he realised he didn't love her he decided to break off the relationship. He'd drunk a little too much, trying to pluck up courage, and Mother—knowing what he intended—seduced him. He began to court Athena, but Mother then told him she was pregnant.'

'With you!' She looked startled.

'Me,' he agreed with a smile. 'And Father, being a man of honour, married the mother of his child.'

'Marina had what she wanted,' Olivia began.

'But she knew she'd ruined Father's life.'

Olivia sighed. 'How sad.'

'She paid for it,' Dimitri said, sympathy etched deeply on his face. 'At first she diverted her love to me. But that wasn't enough. Father never stopped loving Athena. When the marriage became unbearable, he went to her for comfort. She and Father adored one another and were happy together. You've seen her, Olivia. That's the face of a kind and gentle woman, unwillingly caught up in the life of a married man. She wouldn't let Father ask for a divorce. She was content with the situation as it was. And when he died I made sure Athena was secure.'

Now Olivia was sitting with her spine erect, her beautiful eyes fixed intently on him as she tried to untangle the story.

'That day on the boat, the day when you said you stood in the theatre at Epidauros and said you loved me, you had several secretive phone calls—'

He nodded. 'Athena had been rushed to hospital with labour pains. They turned out to be false and I teased her about being a drama queen. Though they were real enough the next day, when you saw us together. That was the day little Theo was born.' He smiled fondly, thinking of his little half-brother. 'Olivia, Athena was all alone and had lost the man she loved more than anything in the world. She needed my support—'

'Of course she did. But Dimitri,' she mourned, 'why didn't you tell me?'

'I had promised her that I would tell no one,' he said gently. 'My mother once accused me of being Athena's lover—she knew where she lived, and I think she'd seen my car outside one day. I couldn't say anything. Couldn't hurt Mother, you see. She was unhappy enough. I believe that when she met you and saw your happiness she was desperately jealous. She envied the intensity of our love. But now she is loved again and her bitterness has gone.'

Seeing how appalled she looked, he moved close to her. Taking her hand, he found that she was trembling.

'Are you saying that I left you,' she croaked in dismay, 'because you were being kind and thoughtful to your late father's lover? Dimitri, I was so certain...' She buried her face in her hands. And then looked up again sharply and he knew the doubts were still there. 'I'm not sure if I dare believe you. You said...you said our marriage was based on sex and that was all!' Her eyes blazed blue fire.

'Not as far as I was concerned. I was talking about *you*. It seemed to be all you felt,' he said, hurting. If she didn't love him, he didn't know what he'd do...

'That's not true!' she protested indignantly. 'I've loved you since we first met! I've always loved you!'

He wanted that to be true. Yet she could be settling for his love, and a comfortable life. That wouldn't be enough for him. She'd told him quite baldly that she no longer cared.

'I want the truth from you, Olivia. No more lies, no more pretence. You've forgotten your farewell note,' he reminded her, his body stiff. But they had to get to the truth, however painful that might be. She must be honest with him. 'You said in that note that when there was no love in a marriage it was a mistake to continue it. You can't deny that. Those words are burnt in my heart.' His voice shook but he didn't care. He was exposing his emotions because this was his last chance to do so.

Her fingers stole into his. He dared to meet her eyes and tried not to be fooled by what he thought was tenderness there. And yet hope leapt inside him, jerking his pulses into a fast, erratic beat.

'Dimitri, I wasn't referring to *my* love when I wrote that note. I meant yours. It seemed clear enough to me at the time, but now I see it wasn't. I believed that you loved Athena, not me. I wasn't going to let you live a lie. I couldn't trust you, and that made every day a torment.'

'But you were mistaken to doubt me,' he said gravely.

'I so want that to be true! I refuse to share the man I love! You must believe me, Dimitri. Whatever happens between us, whatever we decide to do, one thing is certain and you must know it. I love you with all my heart. Don't you know that? Can't you tell?'

It was his turn to hesitate, to doubt. And those doubts haunted him, stretching him on the rack.

'I want to believe you. More than you can ever know,' he muttered. Her grip tightened. He ploughed on. 'But when we were married you seemed so distant sometimes. When I came back from trips abroad our sex was fantastic, but you were quiet. Almost reticent—'

'I was lonely,' she explained, her face earnest. 'All I did was explore the country and shop. I seemed to have no purpose in life except to be your wife. Wonderful though that was, it wasn't enough.'

His arm crept around her. 'I'm sorry. I thought you'd love a life of luxury—'

'Not if you weren't there to enjoy it with me,' she sighed. 'I need to keep my mind active. And I was fed the most awful stories by your mother about what you might be doing. I know you've always denied her part in my misery, but she fed my suspicions. Perhaps that was because she truly believed you to be Athena's lover. I think she might have been preparing me for the truth, so I wasn't hurt as she'd been hurt by your father's suspected infidelity.'

'I'm sorry. To me, Mother seemed so pleasant to you that I couldn't imagine she was being two-faced and making you unhappy. But you must believe me when I say there were no other loves in my life. I slept and ate and dreamt of you. I haven't stopped loving you, not even in those years I wished hell on earth for you. And when I saw you again…I couldn't breathe for the hunger that filled my bitter heart. I wanted to throw that lawyer of yours into the sea, just because he'd spent time with you and on the offchance that he might have…might have…'

'I've had no other lover but you,' she said softly, touching his beloved face. 'I had some dire dinners in the attempt to start my life without you!' She giggled. 'No man matches up. They didn't even come close. I have loved you despite trying to forget you. I always will. But…you…' She bit her lip. 'What about you? You mentioned women…'

'Yes. I went out with other women,' he said, his cheek soft against hers. 'I made love to three of them. A one-off, each time. Such a mistake. A disaster. You were always there, luring me with your wicked eyes, sighing the way you do…' His arm tightened around her waist. 'I suppose it kept Eleni at bay for a while,' he said ruefully. 'I told her how I felt about you. That I was obsessed, addicted—'

'But you didn't say you loved me?' she murmured, lights glinting in her eyes.

'I couldn't admit it to myself, let alone her. I knew you were out of my reach and I had to resign myself to that. Acknowledging my love for you would have torn me apart. I was devastated when you left. An absolute bear. Eleni thought she'd slip into your shoes but I didn't want anyone there. Only you.'

Contented now, she leaned her head into his shoulder. 'She kept trying because she didn't know how you really felt,' she mused.

'Yet she was aware that I'd raged and rampaged about the house when you left.'

'Perhaps she thought your pride was hurt,' Olivia said wryly.

He smiled. 'Perhaps. But…why did you run away? If you'd confronted me, I could have explained—'

'I barely knew what I was doing,' she confessed. 'I hurt so much. Imagine what I'd seen, Dimitri! Imagine the corrosive half-truths your mother poured into my ear! I'd long been unhappy, lonely, unsure of your love and seeing you with Athena just confirmed my worst fears.'

'I was a fool. I left you alone too much. I know that now,' he said quietly. 'I was trying to continue working as I had before I was married. I thought you must be blissfully happy, enjoying your life of leisure.'

'I felt I wasn't part of your life any more.' Her face was sober as she remembered how isolated she'd felt.

'That day when I saw you with Athena, my instincts were to go back to people I knew and loved. My friends. I needed to think—and I couldn't in that oppressive, intense atmosphere. You were in Tokyo, your mother was keen to see the back of me so you could find yourself a Greek wife. And...' She hesitated. 'To be honest, I thought that you'd lie your way out of the situation and I'd be so desperate to believe you that I'd be tempted to pretend you didn't have a mistress and a child. I'm so weak where you're concerned. I didn't dare risk being coaxed by you into accepting your infidelity and turning a blind eye to it.'

'I would have persuaded you,' he pointed out sadly. 'Because I would have shown you the photos of Athena and Theo and there would have been no doubts left in your mind.'

'I know.' She hung her head. 'Sometimes I'm not rational where you're concerned.'

He gave her waist an understanding squeeze. 'I know. I lose all sense of rationality too.'

'Where...?' She swallowed. Could they begin again or had their chances been soured? 'Where does this leave us, Dimitri?'

'Do you trust me now?' he asked. She nodded. 'I am totally committed to you and always have been. I regret my prolonged business trips without you. This time we've spent together has shown me how much I need you, that you must come with me—or I must learn to delegate more.'

'Does that mean...?' she breathed, not daring to say more.

Gently he turned her to face him. 'I love you and you love me. I want us to spend the rest of our lives together. But we must never again be silent about our doubts or worries. Not that there will be any in the future, will there?'

Her smile lit her face with a joy that took his breath away. So he kissed her warm, inviting mouth and forgot everything else.

Some time later they broke away. 'Eleni,' she said anxiously, remembering.

'She will find someone else. Her head was filled with me, but there are many young men longing to love her,' he assured her. 'We'll be kind to her. Give her a party and invite some hunks to adore her.'

'And your mother?'

He touched her soft, concerned mouth. 'She's happy with Nikos. If I'm happy then she'll be content. I think that she will be the mother I remember as a child,' he said contentedly. 'Love will bring out the best in her, you'll see. And we must make sure you're not neglected. You need a project of some kind, something worthwhile—'

'I thought,' she whispered, running her hand inside his shirt, 'motherhood might occupy me thoroughly.'

'Oh, my darling,' he murmured, passionately kissing her. 'Let's have a selfish year to ourselves first. Come with me wherever I go. Be my social secretary. Charm and dazzle my clients. And then,' he said, carefully unzipping her dress, 'we will start our family. For now,' he breathed, kissing her throat, 'we'll just practise our technique.'

She smiled her Venus smile, stood up and slithered out of her dress. Dimitri groaned and held her close. Lovingly she stroked his dark head. Children, she thought happily. Dark-haired, dark-eyed and beautiful.

'Love me,' she whispered, overwhelmed by the joy in her heart. 'Just love me for the rest of our lives, as I will love you, Dimitri.'

EPILOGUE

'EVERYONE on the beach must think we're mad!' laughed Olivia, scarlet in the face from exertion.

'Be quiet, woman, and *hop!*' muttered Dimitri, his eye fixed on the finishing line.

But she was giggling too much. Hampered by the tie wrapped around their ankles as they stumbled across the sand, she finally overbalanced and brought Dimitri crashing down with her.

'Ha!' exclaimed a triumphant Lukas, hopping by and thrilled to be on course to win the three-legged race with his sister, Helen. 'We're the best! Hurray!'

Dimitri laughed and pretended to grab his son's foot, but Lukas was too agile and triumphantly went on to breast the tape held by his proud grandmother, Marina, and his step-grandfather, Nikos.

'The winners!' cried Marina, holding up her grand-children's hands in delight.

Olivia and Dimitri, still chuckling, staggered to their feet. 'And what happened to Eleni?' asked Olivia, looking back.

'Huh. Smooching with Vangelis. And they're mar-ried! Yuk!' said Lukas, with all the scorn of a ten-year-old who knew that winning a race on your birthday was far more important than kissing.

'You'll think differently in five years' time,' admon-ished Athena, hobbling up, still tied to Theo, who was now taller than his mother.

'Never!' Lukas declared.

Dimitri's eyes warmed as he put a loving hand on his son's shoulder. 'Never say never. All is possible. Love will hit you with the speed of a bullet one day, if you're anything like me.' He looked lovingly at Olivia, her arm around their golden-haired daughter. 'And you'll live in a glorious haze from that moment on.'

'Hmph. It's the sack race next,' declared Lukas, dismissing such rubbish out of hand.

'And then pass the orange,' announced Helen happily. 'I'm organising the teams.'

Dimitri perked up, knowing this involved holding the fruit under your chin and trying to pass it to the person next in line. A lot of close contact was necessary, and he had every intention of standing beside Olivia to make the most of the intimacy. He smiled to himself. All these years and he still thrilled to be near her, still found excuses to touch her. Loved her more than ever.

'Men and boys against women and me,' Helen insisted.

Olivia laughed at Dimitri's crestfallen face. She knew what he'd been thinking. 'Save it for later,' she murmured.

His eyes kindled. 'To hell with later. Share a sack with me?'

'Rogue! We'd stand no chance of winning!'

'Who cares about winning?' He swept her into his arms, not caring that his son groaned in despair. 'I love you,' he said, brushing the strands of wind-blown hair from her face.

'And I love you,' Olivia whispered, her eyes adoring, their surroundings forgotten. He held her closer.

'Sack race, Mother!' Lukas was tapping her on her

arm, his face so imperious and like Dimitri's that she had to stifle a smile.

'Are you enjoying your birthday, darling?' she asked, obediently hauling the sack to her waist.

Affectionate as always, he impulsively kissed her and then his father. 'It's great. Quite mad, of course, but that's English parties for you. The cake's *huge*. I'm so lucky to have you and Gran and Nikos, and Eleni and Vangelis, and Athena and Theo.'

Olivia hugged her son and Helen, a burgeoning long-legged beauty even at the age of eight. 'We're the lucky ones, your father and me,' she said softly. 'We were given a second chance and this lovely family is the result.'

Dimitri kissed her. 'Not luck. We were driven by love.'

'Yes.' She smiled up at him.

'They're in that haze again,' sighed Lukas extravagantly. 'I think we'd better start without them, Helen, don't you?'

'Definitely,' agreed Helen. But her gentle blue eyes met her mother's and the two of them smiled warmly, acknowledging their belief in the joy of true love.

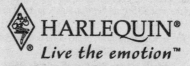

From the bestselling author
of *The Deepest Water*

KATE WILHELM

SKELETONS

Lee Donne is an appendix in a family of overachievers. Her mother has three doctorates, her father is an economics genius and her grandfather is a world-renowned Shakespearean scholar. After four years of college and three majors, Lee is nowhere closer to a degree. With little better to do, she agrees to house-sit for her grandfather.

But the quiet stay she envisioned ends abruptly when she begins to hear strange noises at night. Something is hidden in the house…and someone is determined to find it. Suddenly Lee finds herself caught in a game of cat and mouse, the reasons for which she doesn't understand. But when the FBI arrives on the doorstep, she realizes that the house may hold dark secrets that go beyond her own family. And that sometimes, long-buried skeletons rise up from the grave.

"The mystery at the heart of this novel is well-crafted."
—*Publishers Weekly*

Available the first week of July 2003
wherever paperbacks are sold!

MIRA®

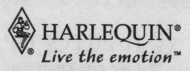

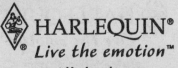

The world's bestselling romance series.

Seduction and Passion Guaranteed!

Mama Mia!

They're tall, dark…and ready to marry!

Don't delay, order the next story in this great new miniseries…pronto!

Coming in August:
THE ITALIAN'S MARRIAGE BARGAIN
by Carol Marinelli
#2413

And don't miss:
THE ITALIAN'S SUITABLE WIFE
by Lucy Monroe
October #2425

HIS CONVENIENT WIFE
by Diana Hamilton
November #2431

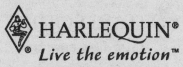

Live the emotion™

www.eHarlequin.com

HPITALH2